Dream On, Brother.
Dream On

by

D J Walker

paperback ISBN 979-8-9874553-4-0
ebook ISBN 979-8-9874553-5-7

December 2022

Part 1 — Mauri's Part

Chapter 1

Mauri Bale had never been interested in her family tree. It was nothing but name after name in small black–rimmed boxes, connected by spindly black lines — skeletal remains with no personality.

She was hard put to give it polite attention for her father's sake, when on a rare Sunday afternoon she found him with his family tree binder in his lap.

And now it was too late, forever too late. Her father had died on Thursday, making his final contribution to his family tree by dying of colon cancer at the age of forty–eight.

Her parents had worked out all of the funeral arrangements in advance. Cancer always provided that opportunity, to face death's details with a modicum of resigned practicality. Mauri had made a few arrangements of her own. She had a tastefully funereal suit ready, which looked so out of place in her closet that she left it in its plastic shroud until she got the call. When the call came she had only to pack it along with a few other things and catch the next flight to New York. She would be back at her job in a few days and, except for the gaping hole created by her father's death, her life would go on as usual. Or so Mauri thought.

Mauri had taken the job in Pittsburgh a year ago, several months before her father's cancer had been diagnosed. She would have taken a job closer to home if she had known that her athletic and fun–loving dad was going to pull such a short straw from the sheaf in God's fist. But not knowing, she had felt free to stretch her itchy wings. She had flown as far as Pittsburgh to begin her accounting career as a junior auditor at a CPA firm.

After the crushing blow dealt by the diagnosis, her parents did not want her to change jobs. Let things go on the course already set, they said. Mauri had thought it over and agreed with them.

She kept her Pittsburgh job, but she visited them as often as holidays and the meagre vacation time of a fledgling auditor would permit. And in between times she amassed what she thought of as her stories, for distracting her parents from the ever more palpable, ever more alien presence of impending death.

Half real, half made up by stretching things a bit beyond, her ongoing stories were mostly about the people she worked with in Pittsburgh. The stories gradually took on lives of their own in the conducive atmosphere of her parents' home in Queens. The parental audience followed her plot contortions gamely, amusedly. And when her brother Stan interrupted his studies long enough to egg her on, then . . .

"Hey, Mauri, I got an idea about that guy you say is always in the file room — the one you think is sweet on the file clerk? Well, now, gas would explain it. See, if a fella has gas, what better place to go when —"

"S'not gas, Bro. Take it from me. That particular guy would never bother to go to the file room for anything like that. He's a master at passing it and then sniffing delicately, as it somebody else just cut one."

"Well, okay then, scratch gas. But I just can't buy the romance angle. I mean, that file clerk's an out and out nut case."

"Um, well, maybe I was exaggerating slightly about her filing methods."

"Oh?! How can you exaggerate heaving a twenty pound box of files out the window? She either did, or she didn't heave–ho."

"Well, she did. She really did. But —"

"And the box either just barely missed the boss man's head as he was going to his car, or it didn't."

"Well, most of the witnesses say that it really landed at least a car length away, but you know how bosses are. To hear him tell it, another inch and he would have collected disability for the rest —"

"And she's still working there? Hey, if you're looking for a romance angle, now there's the place to —"

"No way! It's just that the managing partner has a thing about the firm's unemployment compensation ratio. Nobody *ever* gets fired — but of course there are other ways of getting rid of people who —"

"Thumb screws? The rack?"

"Nah, nah. C'mon. This is the 1990s. They're much more sophisticated than that. The scuttlebutt is that mealworms in the lunch bags of the squeamish have sometimes been very effective, and — oh, things like itch powder in the chair fabric for the more hygienically challenged. Not that anyone's ever been caught at it, but the circumstantial evidence has at times been pretty strong."

"Diabolical. Why didn't you go to work in a clean business, Sis, like maybe running guns for third world countries? Or selling nuclear —"

"Oh, yeah?!" Mauri's chin came up pugnaciously. "You just wait 'til you finish college and get out into the real world, Bro. Then you —"

"Hey, I'm no monk. I know a lot more about the world than you did at —"

"Oh, ho, Bro! No way! Why I'll bet that —"

"Children, please," interjected their mother, chuckling, but casting her glance toward their father, whose smile had thinned as Mauri and Stan's din had increased.

"Yeah, well, anyway," Mauri continued, immediately subdued, "last I heard they're trying to make that file clerk quit instead of firing her. Trouble is, she's got some pretty strong allies in bookkeeping."

"You mean the ladies with so many stuffed animals on their desks that there's no room for their computer keyboards?"

"The same, Bro. Because, after all, the files that she chucked out of the window were for the pet cemetery that got indicted for selling some of the, um, remains as fertilizer overseas."

"Well, I'm no fan of the cute fuzzies, but I can sort of see how — hey, what would you do if a few meal worms showed up in your lunch someday, Sis?"

"I've got that all planned out — not that I'm worried about it, though."

"Yeah, sure."

"I'd wait until one of the managing partner's munchkins was watching and then I'd eat 'em up."

"You would. Yes, you really would."

"Yes. And I'd smack my lips and say that they tasted great and that I wish I had some more. After all, they're supposed to be quite edible — mostly protein."

3

"That's double truly gross, Sis."

"Thanks, Stan."

"Mom, I think you'd better have another one of those mother–to–daughter talks with Mauri. I think she missed the part about the feminine mystique stuff."

"Okay, Stan," their mother said.

"And when you do, could I listen in? I may have some very useful —"

And on and on. Pattering with Stan while one or both of their parents grinned, grimaced, and sometimes out and out moaned. A willing–enough audience of two. A man keen to make his peace with everyone, everything. Weirdly serious — too serious. A woman eddying, oddly tentative, so unlike herself, so unlike water running deep and even, smooth and strong.

The flight home from Pittsburgh for the funeral was uneventful. The plane landed at Newark and Mauri rode the bus into the City, and then the subway out to Queens. She walked up the driveway of her parents' home and rang the kitchen door bell in the back. Such a familiar door, but strange now, a sudden barrier between herself and what was left inside.

Her mother opened the door. It was the same face and the same familiar form. But no, Mauri knew, it was not the same. The being in front of Mauri was masked now, and costumed in sorrow. Mauri saw in an instant that there was a flow of water separating them, and she was suddenly afraid of being yanked and forced into its strong current of overwhelming grief. The image of drowning, of struggling against the water's flow — that was what flitted and wavered painfully around her mother's face, her mother's mask.

"Mauri, dear," her mother spoke, "I was not expecting you until tomorrow at the earliest."

"I." "I" was not expecting you, her mother had just said. Mauri shuddered. Not "we". Not "your father and I." How was it, Mauri wondered, this 'I' instead of 'we'? This 'me' instead of 'us'? But the mask was snug. It fit tight, with no unseemly wrinkles. Mauri could not see behind the mask to the woman who wore it.

Mauri opened her mouth but no words came out. It was hitting her now. The unchangeable emptiness beyond the threshold, in place of the man who had been her father. The man at the opposite end of

4

her being, from her mother. Stretch as far as she ever might, she would always snap back to between them. Distinct or indistinct. Alive or dead.

Her mother's arms opened and Mauri fell into them. The sum for half of Mauri enveloped her, supported her young sorrow. The other half was irretrievably gone, and this present half wore a hideous mask. Inside Mauri something recoiled further, but she knew that struggle was useless. She would have to accept what she had left. She closed her eyes and sunk deeper into her mother's comfortless arms.

"He was better on Wednesday, Mauri," her mother spoke into her hair. "But on Thursday morning he went . . . down. Way down. Then he got quiet. There was a moment of struggle only, and then he was just . . . gone. Gone from us."

*   *   *

By and large they kept themselves buttoned up rather well until the coffin was lowered into the ground. A few quiet tears around the kitchen table, some moments of constricted throat and caught–back sobs among tumbling feelings. After all, people died every day. And the three of them had known that this was coming. Death's dark angel had been encircling their heads for months, and cuffing up against their shoulders. Its foul tattered wings had brushed their faces so many times, whispering the inevitable to them. They had known what was coming and that it could not be tricked away or outrun.

> *O what is this that I can't see*
> *With icy hands gets ahold of me . . .*
> *O I am Death none can excel*
> *I open the door to heaven or hell*
> *I'll drop the flesh off of your frame*
> *The earth and worms both have a claim.*[1]

They hadn't tried to dicker with Death or to run. They had faced it. And then they steeled themselves admirably for the further appalling period of first grief after their loved one's death. Their reward was the satisfaction of an outward show of restraint and acceptance.

---

[1] Adapted from *O Death*, an old Southern country song.

Theirs wasn't the only burial in the huge cemetery that day. They passed two other corteges of late model cars alongside the road to their very own lot number 10754, which was to be the final resting place for the remains of Edward Robert Bale, loving husband and father. The accountant in Mauri automatically tallied the Work–in–Progress against the endless rows of Finished Goods which dispersed over the slopes in all directions.

Yes indeed. People died every day and had always been doing so. And the burials in this cemetery today were a slight surge of wave against the impervious shore of death. There was a vastly heavy ocean pushing behind this small surge. Grabbing the shore for a moment and then coming back again with other mourners in its froth. Death was common, and it would always be so.

But lot 10754 was the only gash in the manicured lawn that mattered when the Reverend's handful of dirt dropped onto the coffin inside it. "From dust unto dust," the deep voice intoned. Then it didn't matter how many other nasty little gashes were in this cemetery, or anywhere else. The entire universe narrowed to the earth clods tatting on the conspicuously unvarnished box lid, a long step down from where they stood.

Mauri's mistake was that she made herself watch the clods bouncing on the coffin's wood. Recklessly she denied herself the glance away, the steadying scan of the rise beyond the huddle of mourners. Instead she persisted, seeking to know more, to feel more. Even if death was common to humankind, it wasn't every day that one's own father was put into the ground.

So she foolishly followed the crumbly dirt on down, and was not surprised, was only mesmerized, when Ma Earth lurched up to reclaim the moist chunks of humus, her sullen offspring, from the coffin's lid. Ma Earth she rose up, and in her crass grab she brought the unwise Mauri down, to be pressed against the lips of her greedy cursing maw. She brought her down into her loamy mouth, conveniently articulated in this manmade pocket for death.

Somehow Mauri's mother and brother were swept down with her, and the three of them were thrown hard against each other in the crumbling oblong hole. Ma Earth's gagging chortles brought a rush of tears to Mauri's eyes, which blinded her in the jumble of arrested movement among the crushed but groping arms and legs. In

6

the awkward roll of three imperfectly balanced torsos came a nightmare of unseemly contortions, impossible to understand, or untangle. Ma Earth tousled them rough, and only eventually did they settle, did they become fixed in a morass of bruised and straining body parts.

They could have laid there, heavily and painfully entwined, for a long time, if their subhuman growls and hoarse brays could have kept better time with Ma Earth's ruddy chortles. But their chorus of wails answering Big Ma back began to falter into coarse ahahags and sobs, and into less convincing jags of choked–off snorts. They knew then that they had lost Earth's close beat. They had to give up the communion with Big Ma. She had tricked them, of course. She had gotten what she wanted from them — their foolish pride — and had retreated, laughing at them.

Mauri's tears subsided with the ugly vocal accompaniment. She managed to rub the smear of grit from her eyes by brushing them against Stan's springy hair, and she squinted toward the light to behold the world above her, the world outside her father's grave.

There she saw an almost perfectly oval ring of faces, pitch black against the bright sky. They were the faces of her family's friends looking down at them.

The faces were carefully passive. The last trace of a gutted sob died in her chest, daunted by their intruding silence. A ferocious anger filled its void. "Do you mind?!" she was ready to screech at them. "He was my father, and we loved him, and we can writhe on his coffin if we damn well please!"

But instead the reticent Mauri, the decorous Mauri, that dominant one of her which sought to go quietly and with dignity in the world — instead that one of her felt exposed under the staring faces, and she strove to retrieve her body parts from the heap that she and her mother and her brother made in this abysmal hole, her father's final resting place. Amen.

It was the Reverend who extended his strong brown hand down to them, to bring them back up again, to life. It was with his help that they climbed shakily from her father's grave one by one, her mother last astride the coffin, silently guiding her grubby chicks up and out first.

7

The military color guard stared coolly into the distance as the family emerged from the hole. No graveside contortions over any veteran of war was going to have any effect upon their demeanor. Mauri liked that. Her father had earned this accompaniment to his burial, which these soldiers were duly executing; he had earned it in Vietnam. The men and the woman of the color guard had already delivered the triangulated flag to the dead man's widow, and they would leave this place at the first viable opportunity, their duty done. What was it to them if the widow chose to begrime their cloth offering with the earth of the departed soldier's grave?

It was the austere distance imposed by the graveside friends which Mauri found harder to bear. There seemed to be no emotion, no feeling among them. These brothers and sisters through the years, most of them from church — now they all avoided looking at the bereaved family, shocked beyond compassion for the time being, by the family's unseemly show of grief.

But there was more. Mauri always knew that there was more. It had been in the Reverend's grip on her wrist as she had scuttled out of the hole. She had read it so very clearly in his patient, but unrelenting, gaze. So long suffering under his own cross. *How could you make such utter fools of yourselves over a white man?!'* she read in his eyes. *'One who isn't even alive anymore.'*

'You're glad he's dead!' Mauri flashed back at him in her mind — but the words were close, headily close, to the spittle on her lips. *'You never liked his white face staring up at you from your sea of brown on Sunday mornings. You never wanted him, albino pale, in your struggling black flock. I'll bet you were even relieved when you heard of his cancer, relieved that he wouldn't be there for you to have to bear much longer — your own damned burden of slavery past. The white man who put his mark upon your race, right under your nose, and dared to sit in your congregation afterward, time and time again.'*

The words were bubbling up and would soon be out in the open. *'Deny it if you dare,'* Mauri was ready to scream. But strong familiar hands braced Mauri's shoulders, and a restraining, "Settle, Daughter," just barely checked her furious words. Mauri swung around abruptly and headed for their car. She would still heed the warm mother voice, would heed the mother's claim on her sullen offspring.

8

Mauri thought that she went alone to the car, but she soon found herself flanked by her mother and her brother. Together they were apart. They would always be apart.

The service was over for them. They were not ashamed. They had discovered the necessary rites and performed them. There was no more for them now in this manicured necropolis.

Mauri became aware that one of her shoes was missing. She vaguely and then with more certainty realized that it must still be in her father's grave. She concentrated on it, a meagre part of herself left behind with him. And she concentrated on walking evenly, with dignity, to the car. Her mother and brother were as disheveled and as streaked with dirt as she was. But they walked with their own silent dignity too.

Her brother slid in behind the wheel of the car. The car doors closed softly and they looked straight ahead out of the front windshield as their car left the line and proceeded slowly down the cemetery road. Soon they would be back at the house. There they would clean themselves, change their clothes, shake and brush dirt from their hair. Some of the other graveside mourners would overcome their shock and would come by to spend part of the afternoon with them. Some of their neighbors would drop in.

By evening her father's life would be formally closed, sealed over. Only unpredictable grief would remain, sagging grief, to be borne in the months and years to come. Everything having directly and physically to do with her father had gone with him into his grave. Or so Mauri thought.

Chapter 2

"Narrative, by Edward Robert Bale, December, 1978.

My grandmother Edwina Bale died at age 90 in October of 1973. A distant cousin phoned me and told me of her death in time for me to attend her funeral in Mirard, Georgia.

It was at the gathering after the funeral that grandmother's sister, my great aunt Madeline decided to give me a 'piece of her mind'.

Aunt Madeline: "You're the boy from up north who married himself a black woman. You're Charles's boy."

Me: "My wife is a pediatric nurse, from the Caribbean island of —"

Aunt Madeline: "It just about broke your poor old granny's heart. And after she'd taken you in and all while your parents were fighting tooth and nail over their divorce. When she heard tell of you marrying a black, 'Edwina,' I told her, 'these youngins'll spite you as soon as look at you. Back when you took him in, it's a wonder that you weren't murdered in your bed.' That's exactly what I told her."

At first I thought that her outspokenness would give me a chance to defend my decision and my wife. It was the unspoken prejudices, I had thought, that were the most difficult to do anything about. But when I told her that Grandmother had in fact written us a nice letter wishing us every happiness in our marriage, my great aunt's eyes got about as hard and mean as I have ever seen in a woman. She sort of laughed and said that my grandmother had never had any spine, had always talked out of both sides of her mouth. "But don't fool yourself, boy," she said. "Your granny knew as well as anybody down here knows, that the white menfolk never take a black woman except for one thing." Quote, unquote. She was clearly enjoying herself — clearly felt herself to be on firm, unassailable ground. I had reddened, and that obviously increased her pleasure. But I wasn't embarrassed for myself or for my wife. What embarrassed me was that this elderly person and I were actually related, that we shared the same blood.

10

I labored on under her flint eyes with our "conversation". I insisted as calmly as I could that none of that had anything to do with me or with my lovely wife. But the smirk on her face, and the way that everyone else was listening but not looking at us — those are things that I still remember quite vividly."

"Mom, what is all this?" Mauri asked.

"Oh, that?" her mother replied. "It's something that your father wanted you and Stan to have. It's the stories about his people, his kin. You've seen the other part I'm sure — the part with the family tree diagrams. Well, he wrote up those stories over the years, in case you kids ever got interested in the past generations of his family. I suppose he wanted to make the people real for you."

"But jeez! Who'd want to be related to this one, this Madeline character?"

"Let me see," said her mother, coming over. " Oh, that one."

"Yes. What a bigoted old . . . witch." Mauri flipped through the pages. "Have you read all of this?"

"Yes, I've read it all."

"I didn't even know that Dad ever lived down South."

"That was long ago, when he was about twelve, I think. It was just for a few months though. And then, your father wasn't exactly proud of his relatives. Certainly not proud of them in the same way that they were proud of themselves."

When her mother spoke obliquely it was an invitation. If you wanted to know more, you had to ask.

"Hmm. Something they were proud of but that he wasn't proud of," Mauri mused, dawdling. She was not really sure that she wanted to know.

This once, however, her mother pushed ahead and answered the unasked question.

"Many of them owned slaves, Mauri, before the Civil War. And a few of them owned a lot of slaves. Then afterward, after the slaves were freed, many of the former slaves were subsistence farmers on their land. And the family had a reputation for cheating those sharecroppers, for keeping them down."

"What a bunch of bastards," was Mauri's reaction.

"Yes."

11

Mauri, Stan and their parents had always lived very much in the present, with the future coming on. Dad had never said much about his family. His father had come up north to be a lawyer, of sorts, until heavy drinking took him under in his forties. Cancer had ended his mother's life soon after that, while he was still in his twenties.

When Mauri was young she had once asked her father why his other relatives never came to visit them. He had replied that they lived too far away.

"But Pappie came all the way from Barbados last year, and he had to fly over the ocean to get here."

"I guess some oceans are easier to cross than others, Mauri."

"Huh, Dad? Huh?"

Mauri hadn't understood then, of course. She hadn't understood his strange talk about great oceans which split up people — oceans which could not be found on any geographical maps of the world.

Mauri had persisted until she realized that her father wasn't talking about real salt water oceans at all, and then ran out to find Ellen. Ellen was her best friend at that time. Meeting Ellen to play at jump ropes was much more satisfying than her father's odd talk about oceans.

By now she knew what her father had been talking about, of course. He had meant the big gapping separateness from people who had no use for you.

The years had gone by and there were no cards, no letters. No phone calls. No visits to or from any of her father's kin at all. And so Mauri came to lump them in with those others whom she discerned that she had no use for. She had her pride. If they had no use for her, then she had no use for them.

"Does Stan know?" she asked her mother, indicating the binder of stories.

"Oh, yes, Stan's read them. He and your father talked about them sometimes, over the last few months."

Mauri's mother paused, taut. Then she added, "Stan wants to go to Georgia after his midterms."

"Why?"

"He says that he wants to see the land that the family place was on, and maybe talk to the people living around there. Maybe find some . . . kin."

Mauri blinked. Her brother, a mostly black boy, snooping around the woods and back roads of Georgia for his white roots . . .

"I think that's a real dumb idea," Mauri said.

"Nevertheless," her mother answered quietly, "he has determined to go."

There was a wealth of subtlety in her mother's answer. Mauri knew from it that her mother had already tried to dissuade Stan from making this trip, and had failed. Stan was going to go anyway.

"Then I'm going with him," Mauri announced grimly. "I'm going too."

Her mother stared out of the kitchen window and let out a breath of resignation. "I thought you might," she said, her eyes worried over her children's youth and audacity. "I thought you .might."

*   *   *

Mauri finagled few unpaid days off from work in late October, for the trip to Georgia. It wasn't the best time to ask for time off, but since her father had died recently there was some compassionate flex.

Stan wasn't exactly enthusiastic about his sister going with him on this trip. He said it was a man thing, that he wanted to go alone.

"So where are we going to meet up, Bro?" Mauri asked him by phone several days before the trip.

"Listen, Mauri, I've already told you that I'd rather go by myself. You know? Having my big sister come along is going to kind of spoil it. You understand?"

Mauri considered and rejected several rejoinders. 'Mom will worry about you.' 'Go to Africa for your buck yearnings.'

"Don't assume that I'm going to be following you around and getting in your way, boy," she ended up telling him. "Besides, we can probably find out more if there are two of us working at it. We'll just meet at the motel now and then to compare notes."

"And since when have you gotten interested in the family lineage, Sis?"

"Watch me, Bro. I just may get rabid about this stuff before we're done. And then there's safety in numbers, Stan. We don't know much about the South, especially the rural South. There's no telling what kind of kooks we might run into in that mosquito–infested swampland down there."

"There're no swamps where I'm going. Dad told me. It was just ordinary worn out farmland. And besides, if there are some swampy patches by the river, most of the mosquitoes would be gone by this time of the year."

"So what are you going to be looking for down there, Stan?"

"Nothing in particular. I just want to see it, Mauri. Walk on the land. See the river. Picture what it was like before, when it was a plantation. Maybe find the foundations for some of the buildings. Ask around about the people. Read the local papers. Eat in the local places. Maybe come back with a story or two to add to Dad's narratives on the family."

"Ah, didn't Dad's stories about them give you enough of an idea?" asked Mauri.

But for the first time Mauri became interested in this trip as something other than a duty to ride shotgun for her kid brother. Stories? Yeah, stories . . . maybe some stories with some kick in them. That was her line.

*   *   *

Stan left from New York and went by train and bus; almost two days later Mauri flew into Atlanta and then headed east in a rental car. Almost five hours after leaving Pittsburgh she was easing the car into a parking place at the front office of a chain motel on the bypass around Gainesboro. The white man behind the counter commenced staring at her even before she got out of the car.

"I'm meeting my brother here," Mauri told him when she got inside. "Stan Bale." The clerk's face relaxed.

"Oh, him. Well now, he's moved on to a different place, further on. Left this address for you."

"Moved to a different place? He only checked in here yesterday."

Mauri listened to the man's instructions to the other motel, her inner ear tuned for nuances. The guy just seemed so pleased to lose both her and her brother as customers. He just seemed so relieved that they weren't staying at his motel.

"You won't have any trouble finding the place, ma'am," the clerk finished off politely.

14

Mauri just eyed him. It was a look she was cultivating for her audit work, a 'Let's get real' look that was supposed to be just friendly enough to invite a telling confidence, if there was one.

But the man just looked back at her blandly. No go. His every move and word had been directed toward getting her on her way. It would take something else to get more out of this one.

They were the only ones in the lobby. Mauri leaned on the counter and turned sideways to survey the empty room and her rental car parked beyond the plate glass.

"Is there something the matter," she asked coolly, "with the color of my skin?" And she waited, concentrating on the deep maroon color of the rental car against the washed out grey of the asphalt.

"Nothin'," came his flat reply. The man was looking at her straight when she turned back to him. "You can stay here if you want to," he continued evenly. "But we do get some people staying here sometimes, who don't necessarily see things the way I personally do. And sometimes that makes for trouble between the guests. Trouble that we'd rather avoid. Naturally."

"Now," he continued, "your brother found a place that suited him better, and he left the address for you, and I've given you directions for getting there. The way I see it, I've done my part."

"I see. Well, thanks for the information," was Mauri's stiff reply.

The guy was just too comfortable with it, Mauri fumed as she eased her car out of the parking lot. He had worked it around so that it was like he was doing her a favor, while he was actually perpetuating the separation, the us against them. And yet the choice was hers, and Stan's. And Stan had chosen to go elsewhere. She wondered why.

Stan's choice of motel wasn't well marked, and the overgrown greenery around the clapboard buildings gave it a decidedly 'out of the way' look. Mauri swung the car into the gravel lot and pulled up to the front building with "Motel Office" painted on its door.

"I'm Mauri Bale," she announced glumly when she got inside. "I believe that my brother Stan has a room here?"

The dark head didn't even look up from the newspaper spread on the counter. "Yep," spoke the head.

"I'd like to speak to him, before I check in. What's his room number?"

"He might not be in. But you can see for yourself. Number 17. Round to the right, at the end."

Stan wasn't in, so Mauri checked in to number 16. Then she sat down and fumed. Stan hadn't left her any message beyond the name and address of this motel. She knew he'd researched this trip and she'd been depending upon him to at least get her oriented when she arrived. But that obviously wasn't what he had in mind. Thanks loads, Bro.

Mauri continued to fume for about fifteen minutes, until boredom set in. She wasn't going to just sit here while her brother was out wandering around the countryside. She got out her AAA map and her copy of her father's binder. "The main farm was large, about 1900 acres in the bend of the Savannah River, east of Mirard."

Easy enough. On the map there was only one big jag in the river east of Mirard. But according to the map there were no roads in that area. Mauri stopped at the motel office on her way out.

The fellow at the desk had finished with the newspaper and was deep in a paperback when Mauri asked him if he had a local map that she could look at. He rummaged in a drawer and returned to his book as soon as he handed over a tattered county map.

Mauri studied the map at the counter. She sketched the one road that ran off into the river bend onto her AAA map, and found that the motel clerk watching her as she folded the map back up.

"You interested in the old Severly Spit too?" he asked her.

"The Severly what?"

"Used to be a ferry there, long time ago. It's still called the Spit. But all of that land has been taken over by the government. There's a nuclear power plant across the river from it, so it's a restricted area now. Nuclear security and all that."

"Oh."

"Yeah. Barbed wire fences and all that. For, oh, ten – fifteen years now."

A restricted area, with lots of security. Great. Well, so much for walking the land. So much for searching for building foundations.

The guy returned to his book and Mauri decided that she didn't like him. He made a show of being indifferent, but he knew too much of her business already.

Mauri decided to drive out to the Spit before it got dark — at least to get as close as she could to it. The weather was closing in when she went out to her car. By the time she reached the chain link fence blocking the road, with the nuclear site warning signs on it, rain pelted heavily on the windshield.

Here's a definite dead end, she thought, staring at the fence through the rain. The fence meant business: it was about 12 feet high and was topped with jagged curlicues of razor wire. Weeds overgrew the gate, and beyond the gate was a dense mass of brownish green foliage.

Mauri had the car in reverse when she saw a white smudge far down along the fence line. A white smudge with dark edges. As it got closer it became her brother Stan wearing a white shirt.

He slid into the passenger side, dripping.

"I thought it might be you," he said offhandedly.

No 'Hi' or 'How are you?' from Stan today. "The only other vehicle," he continued, "that I've seen out here was a yellow pickup that stayed about half an hour and then left. Part of the security for the place probably."

"Seen anything else interesting?"

"Only a way in under the fence."

"Ah, Stan, there's bound to be penalties out the gazoo for entering a restricted nuclear area. Fines. Jail. Bloodhounds. Firing squads."

"Yeah."

Mauri stared at the rain coursing down the windshield. The bottom had dropped out of the sky windows, and even the bold lettering of the warning signs was blurred into smudges by the downpour. She and Stan had come all this way, and if they ever came again, chances were that the restrictions would be greater, the access more strictly limited.

"We'll go in as soon as the rain slacks," she said to the windshield.

"Yep," was Stan's response.

* * *

"It's certainly been a long time since anybody's been through here with a Wonder Weeds Away," Mauri grumbled.

17

She didn't mind the sodden wetness of it all, though there was a distinct chill everywhere that water had soaked through to her skin. They'd parked the car off an overgrown dirt lane well down the road from the fence, and she'd been soaked to her knees long before they crawled through the overgrown washout under the fence line.

No, it wasn't the water that was bothering her. It was the . . . concern about the array of wildlife that would flourish in the dense overgrowth of a place like this. Cold might have killed off most of the bugs, but that still left rodents and snakes.

"They ought to napalm this place every now and then to keep the, ah, weeds down," she groused. "And what's this tangly vine that's all over everything?"

"That's kudzu, Sis. Grows about a foot a day. Some say a foot a minute."

"Great. If we don't get nabbed by the Security for this place, the kudzu'll get us. It'll entwine our ankles the moment we stand still, and nobody'll hear us shout for help except the security guards, who'll mow us down with their submachine guns and leave our bodies to fertilize the next generation of kudzu."

"You've been watching too much late night tv, Sis. As far as I'm concerned, the kudzu is good cover. Only trouble is, all this undergrowth makes it harder to pick out where the buildings were and the —"

"My brother, the archeologist."

They were passing through patchy, scraggly woods on gradually sloping land. Browning now, for the winter. This area probably had been fields once, Mauri guessed. Now it was a very undistinguished morass of weed and haphazard clusters of kudzu–covered trees.

Mauri was disappointed, and she sensed that Stan was too. There could never be any feeling of personal history about this place for them.

The river was an even greater disappointment. They had picked their way through to it, over increasingly rough and uneven ground. It was a murky bloated snake of a river under lowering dark clouds. Flat, idle. Dirty. Dead. Across the river, two huge cylindrical cooling towers oppressed the skyline, looking like abandoned pots on a giant potter's throw wheels. The sides had been swept up, but the final contours of the pots had not been shaped out into any reassuring form.

A chain link fence about two hundred feet back from the shore line kept them from going closer to the river bank, which looked eroded and swampy. A similar fence lined the other side of the shore. Evidently the fences had been put there to discourage anyone from crossing the river from either side.

"I can't believe this place ever was a ferry," Mauri said.

"There used to be a bluff of hard rock along here. You must have skipped that story in Dad's binder, Sis."

"I was going to catch up on reading it tonight actually. I've found it a little hard to . . . to read Dad's —"

"Yeah. Well, the rock was sold to the railroad in the 1930s. A crew came in and blasted it out, and carted it away for rail beds. Some said that was the end of the farm, because the next big rains washed acres of topsoil into the river. Others say the soil was already pretty much worn out by then anyway."

"They must have been pretty desperate if they were selling the rocks along the river."

"Probably. It was the Depression after all."

The light was almost gone and the rain had started up again in earnest. Splotchy at first, it soon poured down upon Mauri and Stan in drenching sheets. They turned from the river and started back up an incline. Their world narrowed a short distance in front of them. Everything else was a blurry haze beyond the rain's curtain.

'What I'm going to remember most vividly about this trip,' Mauri was thinking, 'is this God awful rain.' And then she realized that she and Stan were not alone. Somebody was screeching into the rain directly in front of them, coming right at them. Stan ducked and moved aside, but Mauri stood still and raised her arms, sure that complete surrender to Security was the best approach in this sudden crisis.

"Don't shoot!" she shouted into the rain, toward the screechy female voice that was almost on top of her.

"Hey dere!" yelped a male voice belonging to someone who immediately knocked Mauri down and sprawled on top of her in the mud.

19

Mauri's temper spiked. "You don't have to smother me!" she bellowed into an ample mud puddle, "I've given up, dammit!"

The guy on top of her rolled off and Mauri rose from the mud shaking with indignation. 'At least,' she thought wildly, 'I'm too mad now to be scared.' She glared furiously into the two faces which peered at her just inside her rain–edged circle. A dark brown face set on a thin but sturdy frame, all over slack with surprise, and a pale white face, stern and angry, topping a smaller, shorter frame.

The white face spoke authoritatively under a dripping hood. "Lay ahold of that girl, Zekial!"

"Yes'm," replied the wet brown face.

"Grab her and don't let her go 'til she's locked up, else I'll, I'll give you a whippin'!"

Zekial seized Mauri's arm. "Yes'm," he said submissively.

"You're one of them runaways, aren't you?" the woman accused Mauri.

Mauri just stared at her, unsure what to say. The woman was young — about Mauri's age, but her voice was obnoxiously bossy.

"And I can tell you're a girl alright," the woman continued, "even though you're got up in those men's pantaloons."

This was getting more and more bizarre.

"Thought you could sneak food out from our stores while it was raining?" the woman accused Mauri. "Well, you're fair caught now. And you won't be getting away."

There was something very strange about these Security people. Beside the woman's odd talk, she and the man weren't even dressed like security guards. The man Zekial wore a rough shirt with crude loose pants, patched all over. The woman was wrapped in a dark cape which fanned out weirdly from her hips to the ground. Mauri was just registering these oddities when the woman spoke again.

"We'll lock her in the pen, Zekial," she said. "Bring her with us while I get the key from Aunt."

The woman turned but then wheeled back on Zekial, "And I haven't forgotten that I caught you asleep when you should have been getting in the feed grain. It'll be soaked now and some of it ruined. You're gonna have to spread it out in the shed if it takes you all night! I'll personally see to it that you don't eat or sleep until you've made up for your confounded laziness."

20

The woman drew her short self up with a ludicrous scorn, and turned to sweep ahead of them down the muddy path.

Except that it wasn't a muddy path any longer. It had been, Mauri remembered, when she'd been knocked to the ground by Zekial. She hadn't had time to think it was odd then. But now the rough browned grass that she'd been sloughing through with Stan had reasserted itself. The woman stumbled heavily in it and nearly fell. Her hood slipped and Mauri got a glimpse of heavy ringlets before the soaked hood was hastily yanked back up.

"Tarnation!" sputtered the woman, "Where in creation did all this growth come from?"

Silence then, in the pelting rain. Mauri sensed a marked confusion and uncertainty in both the man and the woman. 'They're not Security at all, that's for certain,' she thought. 'Maybe they're loony drifters or squatters, with no more right to be here than me and Stan have.' She tried to pull free of Zekial's grip but the more she pulled, the more his grip tightened.

"Stan!" Mauri shouted into the rain, struggling. "Help me, Stan!" But no answer came. No help came.

Zekial's grip became vise–tight and Mauri quit struggling. She would have to wait for a better opportunity to escape. She looked full at the man, but he wasn't paying the least attention to her. Rigid, scared–looking, he was staring fixedly into the rain around him. It was slackening now, its fullness spent for a time. Visibility had improved to the extent that Mauri could see some smudgy brown landscape where only a rain–grey blur had been a short while before.

The woman in front of her was intensely scanning the view, like the man.

"Where're the warehouses? The wagons?" the woman queried the slackening rain, imperious still, even in her confusion. "And the stables. And —" She swung around and stared beyond Mauri to the river. "And the landing and the boats! And the sheds by the — oh my dear Lord! Everything is gone!"

Her strident voice had begun to waver. Fear wobbled it, confusion muted it. "Where is everything? Where is everybody?" she whispered tensely. Her eyes squinted and her shoulders hunched forward. Taut, straining to see and to hear, she regarded her surroundings in disbelief.

21

That's when the woman spied Stan in the bushes. That rallied her.

"Zekial!" she screeched, "there's another runaway! Git him!"

"But, but Missus, whut I do wi' dis 'un?"

"I'll keep her, you fool! Now you git t'other one! Git him! Quick!"

Zekial let go of Mauri and ran toward Stan. Mauri leapt easily beyond the woman's grasp and ignored her cry of outrage. She thrashed through the kudzu after the man Zekial. Together she and Stan might be able to get clear of these two lunatics and get out of here.

Stan let Zekial come on, looking like he wasn't going to resist. Closer, closer Zekial came. Then he was on Stan.

And then he was sprawled on his back and Stan was hopping back beyond the fallen man's reach. Stan had thrown him neatly with a one point shoulder throw. Mauri reached Stan's side and together they faced their insane opponents, both in karate–ready position.

But they needn't have bothered with their stances. The strange woman and man seemed to have forgotten them. The woman was staring into the woods, and the man was sitting on the ground, muttering, "Dere be a pile o' chop wood hea. I hep pile it mysef dis mawnin'. Suppose t'be right hea." The rain had stopped, and a grainy evening gloom was closing in.

"The lights were on in both parlors," the woman burst out. "And on the south piazza. Why, Charley Meyer and my Douglas were both in the south parlor when the rain started — when I left to — they would never have left in the rain. But . . . where are the lights now?"

"Mebbe, Missus," Zekial mumbled, more to himself than to her, "Mebbe it be one o' dem big wind tings. Dem cyclopses tings."

"Cyclones, Zekial. Cyclones," the woman answered impatiently. "But that can't be it. There hasn't been enough wind. Surely not enough to sweep everything away."

"Let's go, Stan," Mauri whispered to her brother. "Let's get out of here before these two come after us again."

"Just a minute, Mauri," Stan replied. "I'm thinking."

"Think on the way outta here!" Mauri hissed. "That Zekial guy is strong, Stan, and you won't have surprise on your side the next time you try flipping him. Let's *go*!"

But Stan was staring at the strange pair, mostly at the woman. Her cape was open now that the rain had stopped, and she was twisting a ring on her finger, round and around. The man took an uncertain step toward Stan and Mauri, as if to try to recapture them. But, "Not now, brother," Stan told him in a voice of authority, and then he strode through the dripping gloom toward where the woman was standing.

"Stan, you are cra – zy!" Mauri whined at her brother's back.

Stan stood beside the woman and stared at her close up for a few moments. Her hood was down, revealing her elaborate array of ringlets spilling from sparkling hair combs, and the front of her dress underneath the cape had what looked like real rosebuds pinned to the bodice and skirt. She and Zekial looked like they'd just stepped off the movie set of Gone with the Wind, Mauri thought inanely.

The woman ignored Stan and stumbled toward the woods. The others followed her as she sloughed through the tangle toward where she'd been staring when talking of lights. She came to a halt about twenty feet into the morass, looking completely bewildered. Stan clambered to her side.

"There isn't any house over there," he said matter–of–factly. "And there aren't any warehouses or a landing down where we were. Nothing like that's been around here for years and years."

The woman didn't answer at first, but she shifted her bewildered stare from the gloom to Stan's face.

"You don't talk like a darkie," she informed him bluntly. "You talk like one of those Northern folk."

"I am from the North, and my sister is too," Stan replied conversationally. Then he asked with distant politeness, "Would you please tell me today's date?"

"Why, what's a darkie be wanting the date for? Of all things!" the woman responded with impatient surprise. "Of all the —"

Stan cut her off. "I think I can tell you some things of importance," he said stiffly, exuding at least as much of an authoritative demeanor as she did. "Things that may help you make some sense of all this. But first you must tell me today's date."

The woman's face wasn't cooperative. She'd opened her mouth, obviously to protest some more, when Stan cut her off again.

"Is it really so much to ask of you?" he asked her with an exasperated air.

"I am not used to being talked to in this manner by a darkie," the woman countered, but Mauri could tell that she'd already given in. Still with plenty of belligerence though, she spat, "It's the 29th of October."

"The whole date," Stan insisted.

"Why I never —"

"Please," he said icily.

"Why on earth — well, alright, it's 1859 of course."

"1859," repeated Stan.

"No," Mauri put in bluntly. "You're off by, oh, about one hundred and forty years."

"And you are mentally imbalanced," was the woman's dismissive reply.

"I kind of wish I was," Mauri rejoined, shaking her head. "It would be a whole lot easier than dealing with this."

Chapter 3

Stan pulled Mauri aside.

"They might be genuine, Sis," he whispered to her.

"Genuine what?" Mauri retorted. "Oh, come on, Stan! Time travel is still relegated to the movies and the fantasy books. There's no such thing in real life. Me, Mauri. You, Stan. And they're sick in the head."

"Okay then, where did they come from? Where do they live?"

"How would I know? Maybe they're tramps. Maybe they followed us in."

"I was alone out here for hours before you drove up, Mauri. I'm sure of it."

"Okay. Okay. Then it's part of some weird government plot to make sure we never even dream of snooping around here again!"

"A government what? Now who's fantasizing?"

"Okay, okay. Ah, they're thwarted thespians. They live in an underground bunker somewhere around here, and they practice their acting on anybody dumb enough to get within range of them."

"Then where's their underground bunker, Sis?"

"Well, in a place like this don't you think that the entrance would be hidden?!"

"Then let's ask them. Or follow them."

"Ask — follow — Stan, we should be getting out of here! Before some real Security comes and rounds us all up!

But Stan had that look in his eyes, like he was intrigued by all of this. Stan the scientist. Stan the idiot.

"Give me a chance, Sis," he said vaguely. "Just give me a chance to prod around a bit."

Mauri turned from her brother with a nervy disgust, and found that they'd had an auditor. The woman was unexpectedly close by and had evidently been listening to them. Her stare was still disdainful, still rather wild with belligerence and confusion. But she was also blinking and her face showed traces of a wary curiosity.

"Where do you live?" Mauri asked her. But the woman ignored her.

"I think maybe I can tell you some things of some importance," she said to Stan, mimicking his earlier words in an attempt at haughty sarcasm, "but first you must tell me what you think today's date is."

"It's October 29th, lady," Stan told her, but it's the end of the twentieth century, not the middle of the nineteenth. In fact the year is 199– —"

"You are mentally imbalanced," the woman burst out. "Just menta —" She shook her head slowly and then vehemently, angrily. "How can we even talk to each other if we can't agree on the year we're in?"

Stan shook his head too. Watching them, Mauri was reminded of those dolls with spring–mounted heads that wobbled dizzily at the least nudge. Her head was feeling distinctly jiggly too.

"Actually," Stan was saying, "I don't think that any of us are crazy. Just . . . disoriented."

Mauri snorted softly. Exasperated.

"I know a little about this place," he continued conversationally, "because I'm a descendant of some of the people who once owned it."

Now the woman snorted. Rudely. Then she took a deep breath. "This is a dream, a hellacious dream." she muttered, and then added, in an oddly throaty voice, "Un rêve infernal! Très, très infernal!"

"If you're really from 1859, then put this into your dream," Stan told the woman evenly. "A civil war between the North and the South started in 1861, and in 1865 the South lost the war."

"No!" the woman screamed. "No!"

"Yes," Stan replied. "And the slaves were freed," he added, looking around at Zekial, and then at the woods. "This farm was share cropped after the war, until the 1940s."

"Oh, I must get back to the house," the woman said, rubbing her forehead and then twisting the ring around on her finger. "I must to get back to our guests. Everyone'll be wondering where I am."

"The family lost the farm during a widespread economic crisis in the early 1930s," Stan continued. "Nationwide. Worldwide. The

26

government eventually bought up most of this land and used it as a buffer zone for a nuclear reactor across the river. It's just overgrown land now. Just woods, really."

Zekial lurched toward them. He moved like an automation, like his mind was forcing gross movement into his limbs through extreme effort. Mauri thought he was going to crash into Stan, but he swayed up close to Stan's face instead, with a crazed, topped out look in his eyes and a beatific smile on his lips.

"No slave no mo'? An' dis place be woods? No fiels? No fiels atall?"

Stan nodded deliberately.

"Oh! Lordy! Beggin' pardon Missus, but dis'n ain't yo' dream! Dis'n *my* dream!" Zekial pawed at Stan's shoulders and chest, clumsily caressing this strangely real figment of his slumberous imagination. "Ol' Bette done promise me, she promise me what I dream. I no belief her. No su. An' I still don' belief her. But oh, oh Lordy what a fine dream dis is! What a dream I done git outta my helpin' her."

Tears on his face, body shuddering, Zekial threw his head back and laughed clear up to the darkening sky. His feet came up in jerky spasms and his arms flew out and up and down in a wild dance of overcome brain circuitry.

"Don' end yit, dream!" he yelled at the sky. "Don' ever end!" he shouted, running and yeehawing into the dark brush.

"Dream on, Brother," said Stan toward where they'd last seen him. "Dream on."

"Amen," said Mauri. One of the kooks was gone. Now for the other one.

Stan and Mauri turned their attention back to the woman. Her belligerence and imperiousness were gone. She was weeping now in a way that made Mauri think of a disappointed child. "Oh my Heavenly Father," she whimpered softly. "Oh my dear merciful Heavenly Father. What on earth have you done? How can I be in Zekial's dream like this? How can this be?"

But neither Mauri nor Stan had an answer for her.

The rain dripped on in the darkened place, closing it in with splotches of coarse fog. Mauri thought of the three of them standing in the dripping wilderness, and the image of them as three points on

27

a highly irregular triangle came into her mind. She strove to break it, to break the image into a line between herself and Stan, with the woman as a singular point off to one side. But the triangular image was strong, even to the extent of shifting as the woman moved restlessly, craning into the darkness surrounding them. Mauri shuddered with the cold and wet.

A crashing howling noise approached them. Veering somewhat at first, halting and then starting back up again, it got louder and then broke through the dark tangle. It was Zekial. The four of them became the points of a trapezoid in Mauri's glum imagination.

He came tramping back toward them, gibbering. "Ma cabin ain't dere! Ma wife and ma babies ain't dere! Whea be ma babies? Got to wake up now! Got to wake up!" He swung his head from side to side.

"Ol Bette!" he then bellowed into the darkness around them, "I done now. Lemme come back. I ready!"

The four of them waited, but no answer came to his appeal. No change occurred. Zekial shuddered and got down on his knees before the woman abjectly. Frightened, he reached toward the hem of her broad skirts. The woman stepped back.

"Missus B'sheba, ma'am," he cried out, "Missus can you help me outta dis dream I in? If'n you can I be ever likin' n' praisin' yu fo' —"

In his distress Zekial had come too close to touching the bottom of the woman's dress. She stepped back again in a frantic and impatient distaste. "Zekial," she screeched, "I got troubles enough of my own!"

"And it seems to me, Zekial," she continued from a short distance away, "that if this is your dream, then you're the one who's got to get us out of it! Not me!"

Zekial crumpled suddenly. "I only wanted me a way t' scape! Somethin' a tink 'bout when, when . . ."

Stan squatted down beside Zekial. "You said something about somebody promising you what you dreamt?" he prompted.

"Ol' Bette," Zekial whispered, "she be de spirit lady 'mong us'un. I hep her. I hide her from de patter rollers when she comin' back from seein' her boy wid'out no pass. Save her a big whippin' fo' sure. So she set me t' gatherin' plants fo' her magics. An' den, an' den she tell me t' be tinkin' what I want de mos'. She say I gonna git it. An' I go to the chaff house t' start my dreamin'. But den dis hea rain come

28

on, and Missus B'sheba find me out and is harryin' me on down to get de grain bags in. To git de bags in."

"A–ha!" said Stan.

But Mauri had had enough. This had gone on longer than even the bounds of inanity should allow. And here was Stan, either believing them or egging them on for some reason. But despite — or perhaps because of — her cooler detachment, Mauri had to admit that these two weirdos were good. Whether it was lunacy or acting, they were really good at it, whatever fantasy or fraud they were about. If it wasn't a sheer impossibility, they'd be completely convincing as bewildered refugees from 1859.

But it had to be lunacy or venal acting, or some combination of the two. 'All the more reason to get clear of them,' Mauri thought, and thus she formed a crude plan.

"We can take you to Mirard," she announced.

"To Mirard?" the woman asked sharply.

"We came here from there," Mauri told her, "Ms. — ah, what is your name please?"

"My name? My name is Bathsheba Severly."

"We can take you there with us, Bathshe– —"

"You must call me Missus Severly," the woman insisted.

Mauri ground her teeth. "Alright. Ms. Severly. Our car is down by the, um the crossroad."

Bathsheba snorted. "Your car? You have a rail car? Why, you are a liar."

Mauri decided to humor her. "Our carriage, then," she said.

"You two nigras have a —"

"Whoa there!" Mauri flared up at Bathsheba, "We will not take you anywhere if you refer to me or Stan as a nigra again, or as a darkie! My name is Mauri, and my brother's name is Stan, and if you want to call us anything else it'd better be either person, or human, or, or — African–American!"

"Well, I never!" exclaimed Bathsheba. "Of all the uppity —"

"Af'can what?" asked Zekial, seemingly completely confused.

But Mauri pressed on with her plan. "You say that this place isn't anything like what you think it should be," she said. "So maybe if you come to Mirard with us you'll find some things you recognize, or some people who you know."

29

"Yeah, Zekial," Stan added, "and maybe you'll find your, um, your babies."

"Shut up, Stan," Mauri growled, but it was too late.

"Ma babies," whispered Zekial. "Ma babies." He grabbed Stan's arm. "I goin', Stannie," he said. "I goin' wid you."

"Oh, nuts," Mauri sighed.

She had not really expected either of them to want to go with her and Stan to Mirard. She'd proposed it only to segue out of whatever game they were playing. Surely they wouldn't want to come to Mirard, where they would be recognized and exposed as either looneys or as rabid thespians. Fakes either way.

But if they really came with them . . . well, at least she and Stan would be getting out of this place before any more freaks showed up. She turned to Bathsheba. "Well, Ms. Severly," she asked her, "Are you coming with us or not?"

"How do I know that this isn't some kind of dastardly trick?" Bathsheba asked suspiciously, nervously. "How do I know you aren't going to take me somewhere and do something . . . something just awful to me?"

Stan laughed and Bathsheba turned toward him. He swept his arms in a wide circle. It was full dark now, with only a thin light from a partial moon. The heavy rain clouds had passed on. "Lady," Stan asked Bathsheba, "just what do you think that we could do to you anywhere else, that we couldn't do to you right here?" Then he turned his back on her. "Come on, Zekial, Mauri," he said. "It's this way, I think."

The three of them started through the dark jumble of dripping kudzu, but before long a thin, "Don't you dare leave me out here all alone!" reached them from the gloom behind them.

The four of them then struggled through the underbrush in almost complete darkness. Mauri and Stan didn't recognize any of the trees and bushes that they'd passed on their way in. Without plan or comment, Zekial gradually came to take the lead.

"Dat dere's de drinkin' gourd," Zekial muttered to Mauri and Stan after reading the sky. "Nauth. So de road'll be dat way." They followed him, and they eventually did stumble onto the overgrown road bed.

Bathsheba kept turning back, peering down the overgrown road toward the river. She lagged behind the others, complaining that the bottom of her dress and her shoes were being ruined. But the other three couldn't get terribly interested in her predicament. Only Mauri bothered to point out that she was mostly dry under her long full cape, while the rest of them had been soaked through in the downpour and were distinctly chilled.

"It's actually my sister Rachel's rain cape," Bathsheba said worriedly, apparently willing to confide in anyone at this juncture. "Rachel and I were entertaining our beaus when the storm broke. Rachel and I were just about to start another duet on the pianoforte when —" a self–pitying whine became evident in her voice "— when the rain started and Aunt Mary asked me to check to make sure Zekial had the grain in." The put–upon whine in Bathsheba's voice became very distinct. "And now here I am in Zekial's mad dream with the most uppity ni– — with the most uppity persons I have ever had the misfortune to come across."

It was easy for Mauri to think of several biting retorts. But she held her tongue. They were approaching the gate across the road and the fence line.

Zekial and Bathsheba braved the undergrowth to get close to the fence gate, and Zekial reached out and ran his fingers over it wonderingly. He curled his fingers through the chain links and pulled and pushed at it.

"Whut dis hea net be made of?" he asked.

"Metal rods, woven in and out," Stan answered absently, looking down the fence line toward where the washout would be. But Mauri watched Zekial and Bathsheba closely. If they'd ever seen a chain link fence before, then they sure weren't giving it away now. For the first time since she'd met them, she let herself wonder for a moment if they really were from 1859.

"We'd better be quiet along here," Stan told Zekial and Bathsheba. "We're in a, ah, restricted area. If headlights come up the road beyond the fence, then duck quick and hide in the bushes."

"I don't even know what a headlight is," complained Bathsheba. "And why," she added querulously, "should I have any reason to hide in the bushes? My father owns this land! It's all *his*!" But her voice had lost its certainty, and she peered into the darkness on either

31

side of the road, again turning the ring on her finger round and round.

"Maybe he owned it at one time," Stan answered her, not unkindly. "But I'm telling you that he doesn't anymore. If you want to come with us, then you'll have to duck if a light gets shined into here."

Reluctantly, Bathsheba nodded.

The four of them fought their way through the kudzu along the fence line. Even in her apparent wretchedness, Bathsheba queried them in fits and starts about the rapacious vines. Stan painstakingly tried to satisfy her irritable and irritating curiosity. "A lot of scientists have been studying it for years and years, trying to devise a way to eradicate it," Stan was saying.

"Do tell," Bathsheba said, sounding relatively fascinated, and asked another question about it. Mauri envied the girl for a moment. She was able to keep her mind on kudzu, of all things, instead of this surreal situation.

But Stan had found the overgrown washout and was crawling through it. Zekial followed him and Mauri was about to when Bathsheba bleated, "But I can't go under there in my dress! My hoops'll catch!"

"Can you take them off?" Mauri asked her querulously.

Bathsheba looked shocked. But then, "Well, I suppose so," she quavered, "if you'll untie me." She positioned herself so that she and Mauri were facing the fence when she lifted the back of her cape and skirt to her waist. Zekial was looking away into the darkness and up at the sky, but Stan was watching them dispassionately through the fence. In a glance he and Mauri had a rapid exchange.

'They're very believable, Sis.'

'I still don't believe it.'

'But you're starting to.'

'No way!'

'You are.'

Bathsheba took Mauri's attention then. "The bows are knotted, to keep them from pulling loose." Mauri fumbled with the tie strings until they loosened, and Bathsheba's undergarment slipped off her hips and collapsed into a frothy cloth circle around her ankles. Bathsheba stepped clumsily out of the circle and Mauri picked it up.

32

Its circular rims were stiffened by some kind of flexible rods running through fabric sleeves. Mauri inspected the seams and edges as well as she could in the scant moonlight.

"Handmade," she reported quietly to Stan, "It's all stitched by hand."

They hid the undergarment in some kudzu, and Mauri joined Stan and Zekial on the other side of the fence. Now it was Bathsheba's turn to come through. But she rose up too soon in her efforts to keep her skirts and cape more clear of the wet, and her hair and cape snagged in the bottom of the fence.

Stan was closest and reached down to free her from the fence teeth. But Zekial gasped and Bathsheba screeched hysterically, "Don't touch me!"

Stan straightened up. "Why not?" he asked her.

Bathsheba struggled against the fence and the kudzu, entangling herself further. "The girl will help me," she ordered from her precarious position.

"No, I won't," Mauri stated flatly. "I don't like the way you said that, or the way you just screeched at my brother. He's offered you his help, and he can help you at least as well as I can."

"You don't understand anything atall," Bathsheba whined. She struggled some more to free herself, and then gave up. "Alright," she told Stan, "you can help me."

But, "Hol' up, Stannie," Zekial warned as Stan reached down again with a bemused shake of his head. "Bes' leave her dere an' let de whites hep her. You 'um git whupped real bad, maybe kilt, for' layin' hans on a white missus."

Bathsheba glared at Zekial. "And just where are there going to be any whites to help me in this here dream of yours, Zekial?" she rasped at him.

Zekial still shook his head worriedly, but Stan said, "I'll take my chances, Zekial," and he squatted near Bathsheba to free her hair and cape from the fence.

It took a while. Her struggles had forced her hair and the cloth of her cape's hood well into the turned–back ends of the fence wire. Mauri hugged her sides in a vain attempt at warmth, and Zekial muttered about how you could never trust whites. "She turn on you sure 'nuf, when she wid de whites again," he warned Stan.

33

"Just a little more now," Stan said at last, and Bathsheba's hair and cape pulled free of the fence. Stan grabbed her upper arms and then one of her hands to guide her the rest of the way through the washout. "Lordy!" Zekial expostulated, staring at them. Everything about him registered his extreme reaction to what he was seeing. Mauri simply stared at Bathsheba's hand in Stan's, white against brown. She'd seen her parents' hands that way so many times, but this was different. It was fraught with differences in these totally strange circumstances.

Stan dropped Bathsheba's hand as soon as she was steady and he headed off down the fence line toward the road. Mauri and Zekial followed him wordlessly, and Bathsheba came last. Without the hoops under her skirts she had to hold them and her cape up with both hands to keep them from tripping her. She lagged farther and farther behind the others. Mauri hoped that she was thinking about breaking away from them at her first opportunity. If so, then good riddance!

When they reached the road they walked down the packed gravel until reaching the blacktop at the first crossroad. There both Zekial and Bathsheba seemed fascinated with the silvery grey asphalt in the scant moonlight. They strained their eyes at it and touched it, and stamped it with a convincing display of wonder. Mauri's creepy feeling of the impossible perhaps being real assaulted her anew. I'm getting drawn into this, she worried to herself.

Headlights in the distance interrupted the blacktop examination and Mauri's thoughts.

"It's probably the security guards!" Stan hissed. "Quick! Into the woods!"

He and Mauri dashed toward some woods which were set back about thirty feet from one side of the road. Zekial wavered for a moment but then followed them, catching up quickly, silently, and passing them. 'That guy can really move,' Mauri thought, and she noticed also that when they reached the woods he made much less noise getting into it than she and Stan did.

They watched Bathsheba from their position together just inside the woods. She had remained on the edge of the road, peering at the rapidly approaching headlights. Mauri could just make out her working her ring around on her finger strenuously.

Mauri watched her narrowly. Half caught up in the notion that Bathsheba might really be from 1859, she wondered how Bathsheba was going to react to the internal combustion vehicle and its 1990s driver. But still clinging to her belief that the woman was playing an elaborate or an insane role, Mauri searched for the slightest flaw in her performance.

A yellow pick–up truck with a bold Energy Department insignia on its door slowed down as it approached Bathsheba, but not soon enough for the cab of the truck to be even with her. Instead of backing up, though, the driver opened his window and stuck his roundish brown face well out to look at the woman beside the road. From where Mauri, Stan and Zekial were hiding, Bathsheba and the driver's head were backlit by the headlights on the road.

The driver stared at Bathsheba and then around into the darkness. He was wary, Mauri realized, perhaps suspecting some kind of trick, some outlandish ambush.

His radio crackled and he ducked his head back inside of the cab. Mauri heard the murmur of his voice on the radio, and then his head came out of the window again.

"What yu, uh, doin' out here, uh, ma'am?" he asked Bathsheba warily.

Bathsheba had been standing rigid, ramrod straight, staring fixedly at the truck and its driver. Now she shuddered and her profile seemed to shrink to a smaller size in the headlight glare.

"Why," she countered shakily, "do you want to know that?"

The man considered her and her question for a few moments and then said, "S'cuse me." His head ducked back into the cab again, re–emerging after he had murmured into his radio some more.

"My supervisor wants to know," he said defensively, unwillingly. "He wants to know if you're lost or somethin'. There's no houses aroun' here for miles, lady. If you're lost, then he can call de sheriff to come n' fetch you."

"I am not lost," was Bathsheba's querulous retort, but her voice sounded unconvincing, uncertain.

The driver and Bathsheba stared at each other, neither one seeming to know what to do next. Then Bathsheba leaned forward. Mauri could tell from her taut profile that she had come to some sort of decision.

"Tell me, ah, please," she asked, with a shaky but strengthening voice, "are you . . . are you an, an African American?"

Now the man really stared at Bathsheba. Then, "Excuse me," he said and he ducked his head back into his cab.

The moment his head disappeared Bathsheba snatched up her skirts and capes and made a dash for the woods. Beyond the headlights her white undergarments flashed in the darkness. Mauri was impressed by what she could see of the girl's speed and by the utter silence of her dash. She was at least as good as Zekial was at it. And she was well into the woods before the driver popped his head back out of the truck cab.

He listened intently and looked around for Bathsheba, craning up and down the road and alongside it. And then he turned his headlights off and listened and craned around again. But he never made a move to get out of his truck. Mauri then caught fragments of his radio conversation with his supervisor.

"Look, I'm jus tellin' you what she done said!" And, "How would I know why she ask me somethin' like that?" And then, not too much later, "No, I am not! You *know* I'm a teetotaler!"

Not long afterward the truck eased into the gravel road and on toward the security fence.

"This afternoon there were two of them in the cab and they stayed at the gate for about half an hour," Stan informed Mauri and Zekial.

"Do you think that's enough time for us to get to the car and get out of here?" Mauri whispered back.

"Better not to risk it. We'd better wait here 'til he comes back through."

They didn't have to wait as long as they expected. A scant fifteen minutes later the truck came back, picking up speed as soon as it reached the blacktop.

Mauri, Stan and Zekial crawled out of the bushes and regained the empty road.

"Are you coming too?" Stan asked toward the woods where Bathsheba had disappeared. Silence answered him. But a few moments later there was a rustle and Bathsheba slipped out of the woods. She approached them silently, slowly. Her shoulders sagged and her hands clutched at her skirts and cape, barely keeping them from tripping her. Every glimmer of her movement in the darkness evidenced a defeated spirit. Her face was drawn and blotched from crying, and Mauri remembered that they hadn't heard a single sob during the entire time that they'd been in the dark woods, so close to her hiding place.

Chapter 4

When they reached the car Bathsheba was surprisingly docile about getting into it. She just grabbed her skirts and stashed herself into the backseat.

Zekial was another matter though. He clearly didn't want to get into "dat dere ting." He was fascinated by it, running his hands along the contours of the body and squatting repeatedly to peer at its undercarriage. But he balked about getting into it, and stalled by asking a lot of questions.

Mauri turned the headlights on and Stan showed Zekial the engine under the hood. Then he tried to explain how the engine worked.

"There's these frequent controlled explosions inside six metal cylinders."

"Lordy!"

"And each explosion forces a piston rod up, and that helps turn a crankshaft — a thing sort of like a fancy gear, I guess."

"Oh my Lordy Lord Lordy."

"And that is essentially what causes the wheels to turn."

"'Magine that. Lordy!" And then, "An' what dis here?" Zekial asked pointing at the radiator.

Mauri thought that he was never going to stop asking questions. If he really had never seen a car before, he couldn't possibly understand most of the answers that Stan was giving to his questions anyway. She was contemplating an ultimatum, a, 'We're leaving now. If you're coming with us, just get the heck into the car,' when Zekial on his own accord gingerly eased himself into the back seat. He looked poised to jump back out at any moment, but he was — surprisingly — actually in the car. But he scrunched himself up against the door once it was closed, as did Bathsheba on the other side of the back seat.

Stan helped Zekial snap on his seat belts, and explained to Bathsheba that she should put hers on too.

"Cars can go pretty fast, much faster than a horse and carriage," Stan told them both. "This belt will keep you safer in case we have to stop suddenly."

"Lordy," from Zekial.

Silence from Bathsheba, at first. Then she spoke. Weary. Slow. Almost as if she was in a trance. "Mother and my cousin Emily died — thrown from a buggy almost ten years ago now. Horse just bolted at our turn in. Nobody knows why. He run off and the buggy careened. Hit a tree. They were thrown out. Lying so still on their faces when we reached them. Like little dollies. They died instantaneous. Doctor said so."

In the front passenger seat Stan flipped on the overhead light, which brought another 'Lordy Lord Lordy' from Zekial in the back seat. Stan pulled a soggy wad of papers out of his back pack. Mauri recognized the spindly black–rimmed boxes from their father's family tree.

"Your mother would be Esther Elizabeth Cottle, born August 10, 1812, died February 16, 1850," he read after turning through the damp sheets.

"Indeed she was," Bathsheba answered him dully, registering no surprise at the extent of his knowledge.

Stan ran his finger down and across the tree line and stopped at another black rimmed box.

"Here you are," he said. "Bathsheba Bethay Severly, born December 23, 1835."

"Indeed," came dully again from the backseat.

Mauri leaned over and examined the little box under Stan's finger. "Died, October 29, 1859," was printed below the birth line. But neither she nor Stan mentioned this fact to Bathsheba.

* * *

Mauri drove slowly at first, believing despite her lingering shreds of detachment that her backseat passengers just might need to get used to traveling in an automobile.

"I'm starving, Sis," Stan announced just before they reached the outskirts of Mirard and were not far from their motel, "and there's a Po' Sam's coming up on the right."

Mauri was hungry too, but she didn't want to have to offer a meal to their backseat passengers. Stan was more generous. Anticipating her reluctance, he said, "Either way, Sis, it's been very interesting so far," and Mauri capitulated.

Stan turned around in his seat.

"We're going to stop for some food," he told their passengers. "I'll go in and get it, and bring it back out to the car."

Neither Bathsheba nor Zekial made any reply. They were craning their necks at every building and sign that they passed. When Mauri stopped for a red light, Stan nudged her and she turned to observe them. They were peering through the windows as if they didn't recognize anything that they saw, and Mauri wondered if they'd heard anything that Stan had said about stopping for a meal.

But Zekial tore his eyes off the intersection and looked at Mauri uncertainly. "Are we dere yit, fo' de food?" he asked her, and a child could not have looked more innocent.

Stan started explaining about traffic lights, but Bathsheba interrupted him. "I'm not hungry," she said, "and I have no money with me to pay for food for Zekial." When Stan assured her that he would buy Zekial's food, Bathsheba blinked dully and stared out the window.

"This is where Meyer's Lane crosses the road coming in from the landing?" she then asked.

"That's what the signs say," Mauri answered.

"Why, there was a mill here, and the Thompson place. I passed by them just last Wednesday. They've been here for years and years."

The four of them looked out at the intersection.

"Well, they're not here anymore," Stan commented.

The traffic light went green and they were soon at Po' Sam's. Mauri backed into a parking place along the edge of the lot, where they could watch the comings and goings from the restaurant without being readily observed themselves.

Zekial said he'd take some of whatever Stan was having. His and Bathsheba's eyes were fixed on the facade of the restaurant.

Small wonder. Whether by accident or by design, Po' Sam's management had achieved a certain individuality which trended away from the uniformity sought by the larger, more established chains. A number of bulbous kitschy statues stood like irregular sentinels in a brightly lit area next to the entrance, each one holding a sign for a value meal of the day. The standout among these garishly painted, plastic renderings was a towering pink pig sitting back on its haunches in patched overalls. The sign positioned below its leering grin and ample chins was also larger than the others and announced the very good deal of a complete country ham dinner for $5.95, drink included.

"Does that, does that sign about the ham dinner, does that mean five dollars and ninety–five cents for, for one person?" Bathsheba asked Mauri, her voice largely faint from awe.

"Yes," Mauri answered.

"And that's, that's a good price?" was the next quavering question, to which Mauri again answered in the affirmative.

"My word," Bathsheba breathed out. "My word. Why, that price would buy an ample dinner for four at the best Savannah establishment."

"Times have changed, Ms. Severly," Mauri commented. It irked her, but she was getting caught up in this premise that Bathsheba and Zekial really were from 1859.

The restaurant didn't appear to be very busy, even though it was probably the only one open for several miles. Mirard was a really small town — that much apparently hadn't changed, Mauri thought. Still, several people went in and came out of its glass entrance doors before Stan came out carrying two huge bags of food. Mauri wondered what Bathsheba and Zekial thought of the fact that the patrons of this Po' Sam's were a fair mix of blacks and whites.

Someone came with Stan, carrying a cardboard holder with what turned out to be their drinks. Mauri recognized him — he was the desk clerk at their motel. He even had his paperback with him, tucked under his arm. When he and Stan reached the car he handed the drinks through to Mauri, and he looked long and hard at Bathsheba and Zekial in the back seat. Then he straightened up and shook his head solemnly at Stan. "Nope," he told Stan with an air of unarguable certainty. And then he asked, "So, now you gonna tell me what this is about?"

"In a minute. Just another minute," Stan replied.

"Prentis here is going to eat with us," Stan then announced to the rest of them. "Prentis, you've already met my sister Mauri. In the backseat are Ms. Bathsheba Severly and Zekial."

"Zekial?" Prentis asked. "Zekial who?"

Zekial just stared at Prentis.

"Zekial," Stan prompted, "what's your last name? Your family name?"

"Oh," replied Zekial, "Well, um, Stannie . . . now, I not be rightly knowin' 'bout dat. Not be rightly knowin'." He rubbed his long fingers along the rough fabric above his knees. "See, um, I not be havin' none o' dis here las' names. No las' names."

"You cannot be serious," Prentis stated flatly.

"Am serious, su!" said Zekial, reacting doggedly to Prentis's obvious disbelief. "None o' us slaves eber be havin' us de las' names. No su!" Zekial then eyed Prentis and Stan with his head craned forward. "You ums', you 'ums got deze here las names?"

"I'm Prentis McBride," Prentis replied.

"And my full name is Stanley Robert Bale," Stan told Zekial, "and my sister's full name is Maurial Edwina Bale."

Bathsheba's head swung from Prentis to Mauri and Stan at the mention of their family name. She looked as if about to speak, but Zekial shifted suddenly in his seat, agitated.

"Mister Prentis, su," he asked, "be yu from aroun' here?"

"I've lived here all my life, Zekial," Prentis replied.

"Ah. Well den, su, I'm a wondrin' if yu hear tell o' two lil' dar–
— uup! I mean now, two lil' Af'can Mercans chilluns, names o' Tabitha an' Moses. Yes, su. Now Tabitha, she be eight years, a right sturdy gal but gettin' up a lil' too biggetty sometime. Sometime be a lil' too fine fo' a dar– — fo' Af'can Mercans. An' now Moses, he be almos' five years, a reg'lar lil'ox. Reg'lar ox of a boy."

Uncertainties, anxieties were in Zekial's eyes as he spoke, but he labored on, seemingly unable to stop himself. "Dey be with dere mother, woman by de name o' Janie, n' Janie be where Tabitha get her biggetty ways. Now, Janie'd be a tall un, 'cept her legs sprung some. An' she be one o' dem moufy ones. Yu be always a hearin' dat one, eben haf mile off on de clear days when her mouf really git goin'. Now yu tink yu be knowin' dem, su? Yu be seein' dems aroun' dis here country?"

Prentis stared back at Zekial, as if not knowing what to make of him. But he answered without a trace of his disbelief in his voice.

"No, Zekial. I'm sorry, but I can't think of any set of mother and two children around here who'd match those names and descriptions."

Zekial's head bobbed distractedly and a thin whining came unconsciously from his throat. "Oh," he then said sadly. "Oh. Well den. Thanks yu de same, su. Thanks yu."

While Mauri finished unpacking the food, Stan accompanied Prentis back to his car, which was across the lot. Mauri could see that Stan was doing most of the talking, while Prentis's manner was consistent with a cool disbelief.

Prentis drove his car over and backed into the slot next to Mauri's. With their adjacent car windows open, the meal began in earnest.

Mauri and Prentis kept up a reserved, observing silence, but Stan took on the role of host, treating Bathsheba and Zekial as if they knew about as much as a raw space alien would know about the 1990s on Earth. He helped Zekial unwrap his food and arranged it in his lap. He handed Bathsheba a soda that he had bought for her, all the while keeping up a nearly constant patter of explanations. Zekial had to be cautioned when he squeezed his drink cup too hard and nearly burst its lid off. Zekial and Bathsheba listened to most of Stan's explanations in silence, dumbstruck.

Their awe deepened when they came to examine the clear plastic bags that Zekial's knife and fork came in. After the utensils had been removed, Bathsheba fingered the bags gingerly.

"Not stretchy enough for rubber," she mused. "Not brittle enough for glass. And it's not woven." She held the thin membrane up to the overhead light and poked a finger at it.

"It's plastic," Stan told her through a mouthful of lasagna. "And there's a lot of it everywhere now." A tiny snap at Zekial's lap soon followed.

"Ma knife done broke," Zekial said, holding it up to the light.

43

"S'plastic too," Stan volunteered. "Uh, Zekial, don't you want to use your, um, fork?"

"Dey's fo' white folks."

"Well, not anymore. But you can use your fingers if that's what makes you, um, happy. But don't worry about the broken knife, Zekial. We always throw them away when we finish eating anyway. Here's another one."

Stan evidently felt he'd done enough explaining for a while, so he lobbed one over to Prentis.

"Prentis, how would you explain what plastic is to somebody who'd, um, never seen it before?"

Prentis masticated some food slowly, thoughtfully. The silence lengthened until Mauri thought that he wasn't going to provide an answer. But then, "Well, there's several different kinds," he intoned, "but essentially they are all organic polymers, which in turn are substances with monomers combined by chemical bonds into repeating chains or networks that include carbon and hydrogen. Most are synthetic or semisynthetic, made from petrochemicals, and can be shaped when soft and then hardened to retain their shape."

This time there were four dumbstruck faces instead of two.

"I'm a chem major at Georgia U." Prentis explained, somewhat defensively, to Mauri and Stan. "What'd you expect me to say? That it was conjured from a magic potion by some voodoo queen? As it was, I've simplified it considerably for you."

It was during this meal that Mauri gave up the last shreds of her rabid thespian theory. And she could no longer credit her idea that Bathsheba and Zekial were just plain nuts: even a lunatic would know what plastic was. As much as her practical, logical nature resisted it, she reached the conclusion that these two really were time travelers — that they had somehow managed to walk out of 1859 and into the 1990s.

Silence reigned after Prentis's oration on plastic, until Bathsheba asked Prentis a question.

"Mr. McBride, I was wondering if you are familiar with some of the more prominent families around here who are not, ah, African Americans?"

"Well, yes," Prentis replied. "I probably am. After all, Mirard was only about 500 people at the last census."

44

"The last census . . . which was, ah, when?"

"1990."

Bathsheba sighed. She then named half a dozen names. None of them matched anyone Prentis knew of, but for a few of them he said that there were people in the area who had those surnames.

"And what about my family name, Severly?" Bathsheba asked.

"Tell you what," Prentis replied. "I've got to get back to the motel now. Why don't you all come along and have a talk with my grandfather? His memory goes back a ways, and he might be able to help you with some of those names that you're interested in."

Mauri explained to Zekial and Bathsheba that she and Stan were staying at a motel and that they were going there next, unless either Zekial or Bathsheba wanted to be dropped off somewhere else first. There was an uneasy silence in the back seat, and then Zekial spoke. "I don' be knowin' where else t'go atall," he told Mauri. Bathsheba asked if a motel was the same as a hotel, and when answered in the affirmative, also said that she wanted to go with them, though she said it nervously.

Mauri nodded and sighed.

They were gathering up the debris from their meal when a Sheriff's car rolled into the lot.

Chapter 5

"That's Deputy Sheriff Welson," Prentis told the others. "Act natural, and he'll be less likely to stop and poke his nose into your business."

But either they failed to act natural enough, or Officer Welson was inclined to stop anyway. He pulled up, blocking both Mauri's and Prentis's cars, and he peered into Mauri's car. His gaze stalled on Bathsheba in the back seat, and from the expression on his face Mauri, Stan and Prentis had no doubt about what was going through his mind. A white girl in the backseat of a car with three blacks, all of them strangers. He obviously wasn't pleased.

"Evening, Prentis," Officer Welson said.

"Evening, Tom," was Prentis's unenthusiastic reply.

"Down from the University for the weekend?"

"Yep."

"Friends of yours from school?" Officer Welson asked, jerking his head over at Mauri's car.

Prentis didn't answer directly. "Officer Welson," he said stiffly, "in the front seat is Mauri and Stan. Backseat is Bathsheba and Zekial."

Officer Welson looked the group over again, taking his time. It was clear that he had the full measure of a local lawman's distrust of outsiders, especially college blacks and their white cohorts. His blue eyes measured each of them, shrewd and intelligent within the confines of his agenda, which was to actively discourage them from visiting or — God forbid — settling in or anywhere near his town.

His gaze prodded each of them in turn, deliberately, attempting to maneuver them into the discomfort that would further his goals.

Mauri and Stan returned his gaze evenly, each in turn, but Mauri was nonetheless impressed by the caliber of the man's stare. The guy clearly had the knack for it. Probably practiced it, like she practiced her 'Let's get real,' look for her audit work.

46

When Officer Welson's gaze shifted to the back seat, Mauri couldn't help herself. She turned half around in her seat to watch the effect back there.

Zekial got it first, and his eyes grew troubled and then frightened. Hunted. Devalued. He scratched his ear. He rolled his shoulders. He flexed his legs up and down. An unconscious whine gurgled in his throat. He was suffering. His lifetime of being a white man's animal made him no match for this small town lawman's stare. His nameless fears were unsettling his limbs and mind.

He was actually a strong man, Mauri thought, to withstand the lawman's gaze as well and as long as he did. But his strength was rapidly ebbing. He bobbed slightly in his seat. The pitch of his whine rose, whistling sharper between clenched teeth.

Officer Welson didn't know why his gaze was so effective with this particular piece of black humanity, but he was grimly pleased. His lawman's instinct had already told him that the guy was probably harmless — only a singularly nervous man. But he was prepared to pursue his unaccustomed success as far as he could, if only to discomfit his next victim — the white lover of blacks in the back seat.

Zekial's arms spasmed and his throat whistle became labored breath. His eyes fluttered — though still caught in Officer Welson's gaze — and spittle bubbled at the corners of his mouth. His body began to convulse, bobbing upward.

That's when Bathsheba leaned way over to break the eye contact between Zekial and the lawman. Her own glare met Officer Welson's. "Why on earth," cut her voice, weirdly harsh coming from her smooth, ringlet–framed face, "are you staring so hard at my ni– — my ni– — at my . . . my, my, my person?!"

The officer kept his high wattage gaze on her, but she was more than his match in gazes and stares. And she had just said something distractingly odd.

"Your what, lady?" he asked curtly, with his obvious disgust for her in his voice.

"I mean my human — I mean my frie–, my frie–, my friend here." She spluttered it, reaching to get out the substitute word that she'd seized upon in her rush to speak in 1990 terms. But she still managed to snap it at the lawman impudently.

47

Officer Welson was temporarily speechless and his gaze faltered for a moment. But then his eyebrows worked ominously. The war of wills between him and this trashy girl was *on*.

But then it was interrupted. "Seems to me, Officer," Prentis broke in, "that my friends and I should be getting back to the motel now. Seems to me that we're entitled to return to the motel without, without harassment."

"Shut up, Prentis," Welson growled. But he did not renew his stare. Instead he brought a small black notebook up to his steering wheel and opened it to a blank page.

"You all will kindly give me your names and addresses, starting with the female in the back seat," he ordered.

"Well, I'd just rather not," Bathsheba retorted furiously. "Because we're, we're not doing anything wrong here. Are we?"

"And um, what reason do you have for wanting to know their names?" Prentis asked.

"I'm investigating a report," Office Welson replied sanctimoniously, "a report of a strange white woman in a prom dress said to be out wandering the back roads. So it seems to me I've got grounds for getting all of your names, particularly the, ah, lady in the back seat.

"An' if you want to argue with me about it," he grated at them, "I may feel the need to call in reinforcements, and to escort you all down to the station."

"I'll give you my name then," Bathsheba snapped. "But I assure you, sir, that I'm not accustomed to being spoken to in this manner!"

Officer Welson merely waited, pen poised.

"My name is Bathsheba Bethay Severly."

"Bath? Bath — what?" Officer Welson asked, frowning.

Bathsheba spelt her name for him. "It's from the Bible. All of us were named from the Bible," Bathsheba sniffed. "Bathsheba was an Old Testament woman. King David had her husband killed so that he could have her for himself."

"Do tell," the lawman said coldly. "Well, then, Bathsheba —"

"You can call me Miss Severly if you want to talk to me," Bathsheba insisted.

"Alright. Ms. Severly, I'll have some identification."

"If you don't mind," he added with more than a trace of sarcasm.

"But I do mind," Bathsheba retorted. "I don't have any identification with me," she asserted in a haughty tone, daring the lawman to do anything about it.

Mauri dove in.

"I'll vouch for both her and Zekial, Officer," she told him, trying to use a bossy tone similar to Bathsheba's. "I have plenty of identification with me."

The officer collected Mauri and Stan's names, addresses and occupations. He minutely examined Mauri's driver's license and her employee card, and Stan's Fordham student I.D.

"Bale . . . Bale," he drawled. "Now that used to be a pretty big name in these parts, at least among the, uh, white folks."

The prudent thing to do would have been to make no reply. But Mauri plunged in again. "One of our grandfathers," she said crisply, "was, um . . ."

"Stanley Edward Bale," Stan supplied.

"He grew up in this area," Mauri continued, "and we probably have lots of white kin living around here. But there hasn't been hardly any contact with them since our white father married our African American mother in 1974." A catch of breath escaped from Bathsheba in the back seat.

"So you would be Ed Bale's kids," Officer Welson said. The fact didn't seem to please him. He looked like he had smelled a bad smell. "Met him once or twice, when he stayed with his grandmother one summer. Long time ago now."

"He died last month," Stan put in.

"Shame," Officer Welson stated, but he didn't sound like he meant it. "Shame," he repeated idly.

The officer handed back the identification and shifted his attention to Zekial.

"Full name," he prompted.

"It's, um, Zekial. Zek–, um Zekial."

"His name is Zekial Abraham Porter," Bathsheba informed the lawman grandly, snappishly. "And he isn't carrying a stitch of identification either."

"I'll thank you to let Mr. Porter answer for himself," Officer Welson snapped.

49

"Well it's a wonder he can remember his name atall, after that staring down that you gave him!" Bathsheba rejoined. 'A good offense is the best defense,' Mauri thought of Bathsheba's attitude.

The blue eyes under the raised eyebrows of the law locked again with the blue eyes of the ringleted girl, and both pairs darkened waspishly. Both were easily capable of being stubborn beyond reason, but the girl's eyes won out this time, probably because she knew she had the most to lose.

"Well then," Officer Welson growled sourly, shifting his attention to his notebook, "and just where are you two from?"

"We both come from a . . . farm, a farm upriver," Bathsheba answered brightly after a pause, in an oddly companionable tone. "About, oh, fifty miles from here, I reckon. North of Augusta. County of Columbia. Severly used to be a big name up that way, but seems as there aren't so many of us around anymore. C'est la vie, n'est pas?" Bathsheba added with a sigh.

"Say la what?" asked Officer Welson, surly.

"It's French," purred Bathsheba with a sweet smile and a coy purse in her lips.

Mauri couldn't believe it. Bathsheba had switched from a waspishly angry harridan to a shameless flirt in seconds. The effect was bizarre. Zekial gaped at her, and her other companions were appalled, sensing that this wasn't the right approach to take with the lawman. At best it was demeaning and embarrassing.

Officer Welson himself looked grievously insulted. He clearly had no interest in being flirted at by this weird girl. He snapped his notebook shut and with a, "You all just be sure to stay out of trouble now," and he moved his car abruptly to free them from their parking spaces.

Bathsheba cackled and said, "That'll teach him to be bothering me," when he was well out of earshot.

He followed them in his car though, as they drove to the motel, leaving them only when they pulled into the lot.

"I'll see if Pops can come over," Prentis informed them as he left them at Stan's room.

"Real talkative guy," Mauri groused at Prentis's receding back, "except when the subject is plastics. Then you can hardly get a word out of him."

Mauri and Bathsheba went to Mauri's room, where Mauri offered Bathsheba a change of clothes, on the condition that she drop her insistence that they call her Miss Severly.

"You wouldn't lie to me, would you?" Bathsheba asked abruptly. "Because you don't like me enough to spare my feelings. Tell me —"

"I'd try to spare your feelings whether I liked you or not," Mauri countered, "unless you were messing with me."

"Unless I . . . what?"

"Were bothering me. Angering me. Something like that."

"Oh. Well, all right then. Tell me about the war that your brother said began in 1861, and about the freeing of the slaves. Tell me without, ah, considering my feelings."

Mauri told her. But despite Bathsheba's express desire to know the unvarnished truth, she visibly flinched over Mauri's cursory mention of the burning of Atlanta, and of Sherman's march to the sea.

"Many," Bathsheba faltered, "many must have perished in that . . . war."

"Oh, about 600,000, if I remember correctly," Mauri stated.

Bathsheba closed her eyes. "You seem to know a lot about it for . . . for a girl."

"History was my minor in college. It's Stan's minor too."

"Ah. You went to college."

"Yes. With lots of other men and women. It's very common now."

"Oh?"

"Yes. Has been for many years. And lots of women have careers now — professions — just like men. They don't just get married and have kids."

"Ah . . . kids?"

"Children. Babies."

"Oh." Bathsheba swayed onto the bed and sat rubbing her forehead. "I am weary," she murmured. "So very weary."

She looked weary. Face slack, shoulders drooping, back curved, arms languid. Even her ringleted curls seemed to be drooping.

"My mother would have been pleased, about the slaves being freed," Bathsheba commented through a yawn. "She always felt that it was not right."

"Well, if she ever did anything about it, it never got into the history books," Mauri commented dryly.

"Mm? Oh, no. Of course not. What could she or any other woman have done about it? Everyone would have just shunned her, or derided her. As it was, the dar– — the African Americans were always taking advantage of her. Papa had to intervene many times. It was the one thing they ever really disagreed about. But of course Mama always gave in."

"Oh, of *course*."

Bathsheba barely heeded the sarcasm of Mauri's reply. She spoke in a dull sleepy voice, almost like a self–induced hypnosis.

"I shall look forward to learning more about the Civil War and events since then," she murmured.

"There have been lots of changes. You've got some real doozies in store for you," Mauri commented.

"Mm? Yes. I actually have a keen interest in history, though I've never formally studied it."

"My father was a history buff too," Mauri replied dryly. "Perhaps it runs in the family."

Bathsheba blinked sleepily. "Do you really think of you and me as being part of the same family?" she asked dully.

Mauri had been starting to admire a few things about the girl. And she looked so quaint and out of place sitting on the bed in her bedraggled eighteenth century evening gown. But Mauri immediately felt the insult in Bathsheba's offhand question. The wall of skin color dropped between them. Better to stick with the bare essentials of polite exchange between strangers, Mauri resolved. This girl would have nothing to do with her as soon as she got her bearings in the 1990s.

Mauri got out her copy of her father's binder, and she studied the family tree in it intently.

"It's not a question of what I think," she then stated coldly. "According to this family tree you are my great aunt three times over, even though you're about . . ." Mauri paused to calculate before continuing, "a year older than I am." Mauri snapped the folder shut and laid it on the desk.

Bathsheba sighed deeply. She didn't seem to notice that she had insulted Mauri with her question, or that Mauri's manner toward her

52

had markedly stiffened. But she seemed to be waking back up. She roused herself from her semi–stupor to speak.

"All right, then," it's theba," she told Mauri.

"Pardon? What's theba?" Mauri asked.

"Theba is what you may call me, instead of Miss Severly."

"Oh." Mauri turned to her suitcase shaking her head. This Bathsheba didn't seem to have a clue.

Bathsheba used the bathroom to change and was in there a long time. First Mauri noticed that the toilet was being flushed many times, with an awed, "Well I declare," sounding weakly through the bathroom door after each flush. Then there was a long silence and Bathsheba eventually emerged in some of Mauri's clothes. The fit was fairly close, and Bathsheba had gotten the jeans and shirt outfit mostly right. Only her hips looked bunchy, and Mauri guessed that she had retained some of her bulky underwear.

She had combed out her elaborate ringlets. Mauri suggested a ponytail and lent her a clasp for it.

"A pony tail!" Bathsheba exclaimed into the mirror. "My word, that is exactly what it looks like too. Like a dirty old —"

Bathsheba narrowed her eyes. "You wouldn't be making me a laughing stock, would you, with this here coiffure?"

On her way to the bathroom Mauri assured her that it was very common hairstyle. She picked up Bathsheba's dress and examined. Even to Mauri's unpracticed eye, the dress exuded the era that Bathsheba and Zekial said they were from. The fabric was tightly woven and smooth, its weight belied by a cleverly reinforced bodice. All hand stitched. Its exquisite taste and workmanship were obvious. Perhaps it was more obvious because the dress was sodden and stained at the bottom now. Even the drag and the muddy stains could not lessen the dress's other–worldly beauty.

Bathsheba had removed the rosebuds and put them in a wilted pile on the sink. Mauri fingered them, trying to imagine a world of beaus, and of parlors lit without electricity.

"It had been one of my mother's, made over for me," Bathsheba said of the dress, from the doorway. She seemed to have overcome her drowsiness. "Of course I only wore it on special occasions. The fabric came all the way from Philadelphia. Rachel was quite jealous of it."

53

"Rachel?"

"My sister. Rachel wanted it, but Aunt Mary had it made over for me instead. She favors me, because I help her so much with the running of the house. Rachel never does anything to help out unless it suits her, which isn't very often."

"Helping your aunt included prodding Zekial and the other slaves?" Mauri asked.

Bathsheba's face hardened. "You have to be after them all of the time," she complained, "else they won't do a thing. They're very lazy, and they're all thieves."

"Perhaps you'd have stolen a few things too, if you'd been an underfed slave," Mauri rejoined.

"Underfed?!" Bathsheba rejoined. "Why, they all eat like — we are very good to our slaves. We feed them very well, and we take much better care of them than most of our neighbors." Bathsheba sniffed. "But they are still so ungrate– — why, you talk just like the abolitionist minister I met once, when I was at the academy in Augusta. Of course he didn't stay long, once enough people found out what his true sentiments were. But I can give you the same answer that I gave him. I didn't start slavery, and it's not for me to try to change the way things are."

"How easy for you," Mauri snapped, "how very convenient and easy."

But Bathsheba refused to snap back, and she took on a distracted, oblivious air. Mauri sensed that it was a deliberate pose, an evasion. They had re–entered the main room and Bathsheba touched the television set.

"What is the nature of this piece of furniture?" she asked.

Mauri told her what it was called and cast about in her mind for a way to explain it.

"Uh, maybe Prentis should explain it," she finally replied.

"Spare me that," Bathsheba said quickly. "I didn't understand a word he was saying about plastics."

"Me either," Mauri admitted. "But anyway, plastics and television are just things that all of us take for granted now. They've been around for, oh, about fifty years or so."

Mauri sat down on the bed and faced her triple great aunt squarely. "There have been a lot of changes in the last 140 years.

54

Much, much more than in the 140 years before 1859. If you stay in the 1990s, you're going to learn about things called computers and . . . um, airplanes, and . . . let's see . . . submarines. And you're not going to believe this, but several people have traveled to the moon and back, in spaceships. They walked and rode around in special spacesuits and brought back rocks and dirt for scientists to study. And others have lived in outer space —"

Bathsheba burst out laughing. It was a rich musical laugh at first, but it rapidly plunged into a hysteria of denial, and hiccups.

Mauri grabbed Bathsheba's shoulders and shook her firmly, steadily.

"But it doesn't matter!" she told Bathsheba. "It doesn't matter whether we've been to the moon or not, because we're still a bunch of stupid, warring, back–stabbing humans — that much about us will probably never change!"

It was the right thing to have said. Bathsheba blinked rapidly and a modicum of reason flickered in her eyes. Mauri released her shoulders and mumbled an apology.

"Back–stabbing humans," Bathsheba repeated softly, swaying slightly and nodding. "Back–stabbing humans . . ."

"Let's go join Stan and Zekial next door," Mauri suggested edgily. "Maybe we can do some kind of planning until Prentis's grandfather comes."

Bathsheba nodded a little dizzily. "You go ahead," she told Mauri. "I'll, I'll be along in a few minutes."

"You sure you'll be alright?"

"Yes. Yes. Perfectly. You go on now," Bathsheba insisted. "I'll be along soon."

Mauri went next door. An old Star Track episode was on the television. Zekial sat in front of the tv next to Stan, his eyes glued to the screen and his jaw slack. He was wearing one of Stan's T–shirts and a pair of Stan's jeans, rolled up at the bottoms.

"Uh, Stan," Mauri said, nodding toward the tv, "are you sure this is wise?"

"I'm sorry, Sis, but it was either Star Track or something about witches with Angelica Houston in it, or the news. And man, let me tell you, the news was lots worse than this."

"What I mean is —"

"Lordy!" burst from Zekial. "Lordy!"

Captain Kark, Mr. Spook, Lt. Uhuta and the doctor were being beamed off the Starship Endeavor.

"Oh, that's just another special effect, Zekial," Stan hastened to tell him. "It's another trick with the camera. Remember what I told you about —"

"Dey done disappear!" Zekial wheezed, seizing Stan's arm. "Dey done —"

"And now they're back. See, Zekial?" Stan said, prying his arm free of Zekial's grip. "See, in the made up story, they're on the planet Mabderflee now."

Captain Kark and the others warily scanned the arid landscape, while some hideous looking creatures watched them from behind purple rocks. Zekial gripped Stan's thigh convulsively.

"Hey!" Stan yelped. "Easy, Zekial! Easy! Remember it's just a story, just a made up —"

But Zekial didn't seem to hear him.

"Maybe you're right, Sis," Stan said hurriedly. "Maybe he should watch, um, something else for a while."

Mauri walked over to the set and turned it off.

"Stan," she began, "this is going to take planning. This is —"

A frenzied animal scream came through the wall from Number 16.

"What the — that was Theba," said Mauri, rushing from the room. Stan followed her, but Zekial didn't move. He just sat on the bed and stared at the blank tv screen.

In Number 16 Bathsheba was sitting at the desk where Mauri had left her copy of her father's family tree binder. The book was open and Bathsheba's ghastly pale, stricken face hung bobbing over the little black–rimmed boxes.

Mauri and Stan figured that she had discovered her death date among the boxes. Her wildly staring eyes lifted from the page and fixed on Mauri and Stan as they approached her, and an anguished cry rose up from deep within her chest.

"I'll kill her!" Bathsheba screamed. "I'll kill her!"

Mauri stepped quickly behind Stan. "Grab her, Stan," she hissed at her brother, "Quick! Before she —"

56

"She, she, she . . . she married my beau!" Bathsheba screeched, face suffused purple with hate and suffering. "He was *my* beau! I was supposed to, to . . . and my brother, my brothers all dead and she — my own sister — she got it all. Got it *all!* Oh the slut! The slut! I hate her! I hate, hate, hate her! Aaaah, I wish I was dead!"

Dry, croaking sobs wracked the girl's body, and her face crumpled into a grotesque of misery.

Prentis walked in then, behind Mauri and Stan. "It's a good thing this a slow weekend for the motel," he said, "with all this screeching going on."

Then he added, "Pops is here, next door in 17."

"I'll kill her!" Bathsheba whimpered into her hands. "I'll kill her!"

Prentis glanced at Mauri. "She mad at you about something?" he asked.

"No, thank God," Mauri replied shakily, and explained that Bathsheba had just discovered that her sister had married her fiancé back in 1861.

"That's all?" Prentis asked.

"I'll kill her," Bathsheba moaned. "I'll —"

"You can't," Prentis stated flatly. "She's already dead. Dead for, oh, probably 90 or 100 years now." He thrust his hard dark face up close to Bathsheba's blinking tear–stained one. "But you're alive," he added with an unfriendly grin. "You're alive and she's bones in the ground."

Bathsheba groaned and then sniffed abruptly.

Prentis went to the door and turned back for a moment before leaving. "Pop's pretty old and these are late hours for him. So if any of you want to talk to him, better come now."

"But I won't allow no hollering and screaming around him, Ms. Severly," Prentis added sourly.

Bathsheba sniffed again but got up to follow Mauri and Stan. "It's Theba now, Prentis," she said with a slight sob. "And I promise not to, to carry on in front of your grand–, grandfather."

Mauri stopped Prentis outside of Number 17.

"You're a chemist, a scientist," she whispered to him.

"Going to be," Prentis replied with a thin smile, the first real smile that Mauri had seen on his face. "Going to be."

57

"Close enough," Mauri replied, slightly distracted by the smile. "So — I mean, do you really believe all of this, about Zekial and Bathsheba? I mean, how can —"

"Just come on and meet Pop," Prentis said, opening the door.

Chapter 6

Pop was a tiny old man who looked like he might be about eighty years old. In fact he was ninety–five.

He was sitting in an amply padded chair, a bulky folding contraption that Prentis had brought in and set up for him. Mauri thought that Pop's hands were large for his frame. His twisty, bulbous fingers lay placid on his bone–thin thighs.

"De hans git that way, girl," Pops said to Mauri, "from the fiels. From the work o' the fiels." There was a thin smile on his lips like Prentis's, but there was a deliberate blankness in his dark, sunken eyes. 'Like a mask,' Mauri thought, with the eye slits empty, for now.

Zekial was still sitting in front of the blank television screen, but he was turned toward the old man, silent, his head bowed. He seemed oddly subdued.

Pop surveyed them silently. Mauri and Stan, standing together before him. Prentis behind them, and Bathsheba just inside the door.

"He done tell o' my Tabitha and my, my . . . po', po' Moses," Zekial whispered brokenly.

"His Tabitha was my grandmother," Pops informed them dryly, his eyes blank like dull cold coals. "She die when I'se 'bout thirteen. Afore then — afore she die — she had a tolerable good life, I s'pose for a nigger who didn' go Nauth after the war."

His chair creaked as he shifted slightly in it, but there was no other sound in the room. No one else moved. Pop twisted his head back and watched them all through half–closed eyes as he spoke. "Now, she done tell me the ol' stories many a time. Many a time. An' I hear tell of this here Zekial. Said by mos' to have drown a white girl in the river —"

He stopped there, his eyes on Bathsheba.

"Said to have drown his mean ol' missus," he continued. "She suppose to be a bad 'un, a whippin' one."

59

Bathsheba looked stricken. "I, I did it once, but, but there was —
but even so it was horrible. Just horrible. My aunt, my aunt did the
whipping, mostly. And, and besides, Zekial didn't drown me."

Pops's eyes burned into Bathsheba before sliding off her and
over to Zekial. Zekial was staring at the carpet.

"Yu tell 'em, Mistah Pops," he said huskily, "Yu tell 'em please,
'bout ma boy."

"That was my great uncle Moses," Pops drawled. Then,
"Lynched," he spat. "Strung up by whites in the night, an' fo' what?
Fo' gettin' too biggetty. He complainin' that harvest, see, he
complainin' 'bout the figurin' o' the shares. So he got caught out one
night and end up swingin' from a tree branch near the mill road.
Body beat up, cut up. Rather not say jus' how. But I saw it. We all
saw it. On the way t' church it was. I was lil' then, but I remember it.
Oh, I remember it. S'was real bad, t' see a man done that way.
Terrible. But that was the way o' things then. Way o' things."

Zekial bent over and sobbed. Pops tucked his head down and
rested it on his chest. The others were motionless and silent, heavily
silent in the small room.

Zekial's sobs gradually tapered off into deep chest sighs.

"I'm sorry," Bathsheba quavered in a weird mixture of sadness
and a nervy distaste. "I'm sorry about your . . . loss."

Zekial sobbed again softly.

Pops stirred himself to stare coldly at Bathsheba, and then leaned
back his head to speak again.

"Well, now, let's get back to the story o' this here Zekial. After he
and his missus was gone, mos' everybody thought she drown and
that he got away Nauth somehow, or got hissef kilt on the way.
That's what mos' everybody else thought.

"But my grandmother, she never belief that. For one thing, she
was made to help with the dressin' o' the drown body that they foun,
and she no think it be the right one. An' for another, Grandmother
jus' not belief her daddy do like that. 'I wouldv',' she use to say with
some fire in her eyes, 'I wouldv', but not ma daddy. No su!'" Pop
snorted and his lips stretched over his teeth in a grim smile.

"Oh ma boy. Ma po' lil' boy," Zekial groaned.

"Now, my grandmother tell of an ol' one in the cabins," Pops
continued, "when she was a girl. This ol' woman say she could do the

60

conjurin'. Some belief her, some not. Well, my grandmother always think this ol one have somethin' t' do with her daddy disappear. Because this ol' one was uncommon nice t' her and t' Moses when they was lil', after their daddy gone, even though she and my grandmother's ma didn't never git along atall.

"So my grandmother always feel it, that dis ol' one know something, but she never tell it."

Silence fell, and lengthened, except for Zekial's occasional deep sighs.

"So all this, if it's true," Mauri said to Pops, "would make Zekial your great grandfather, and Prentis's triple–great grandfather."

"I reckon," replied Pops with a thin smile, the first one Mauri'd seen from him with any warmth in it. "I reckon."

Pops let another silence settle in. His eyes were somewhat kindled now, black shimmers in his face. When he judged the silence had been long enough, he directed his gaze at Mauri and Stan.

"So you two," he said to them, "come down here to see your roots. Mmm . . . look t' me you got more than you bargain for," shifting his gaze over to Bathsheba.

∗   ∗   ∗

Car wheels crunched on the gravel outside and headlights flung a pattern across the far wall of Number 17. Prentis went to one of the windows and peered out.

"Two sheriff cars," he announced. "Officer Welson getting out of one of them. Office Burns from the other with . . ."

He paused to identify someone. "With Clarence," he finished.

Car doors slammed and footsteps approached.

"Door's open," Prentis called out, and the two sheriff officers and the man Clarence entered the small room. Mauri recognized Clarence: he was the guy in the Energy Department truck whom Bathsheba had spoken with near the crossroad. He looked uncomfortable now, and avoided looking at everyone except Pops. Pops eyed him silently, his face a blank mask again. Clarence nodded slightly and dropped his eyes to the carpet.

The room was too full of people, and in the shifting to fit Bathsheba deliberately arranged to be standing next to Officer Welson.

"Evening, Mr. Porter," Officer Welson said to Pops. Pops just stared at him. "Evening," Officer Welson said to the rest of them. "This here's Mister Clarence Smith."

"Clarence," he asked, "do you recognize anyone in this room?"

Clarence looked at each person in turn. When he looked at Bathsheba she just gazed back at him and stifled a yawn.

Clarence returned his eyes to the carpet before he spoke. "I rec'nize Pops n' Prentis. Das all," he said. But he was a bad liar. His shoulders hunched and he blinked at the carpet unhappily.

"You sure?" Officer Welson asked sharply. "Clarence, this here white woman's changed her hairdo some, but with lots of curlicues all around her face she would match the description you —"

"Leading the witness, Officer?" Mauri put in.

Officer Welson's eyes swiveled around to regard Mauri, but before he could speak, "Maybe you're looking for my sister Rachel," Bathsheba cut in, at his elbow.

"Your who?" Officer Welson rounded on her and almost bumped into her, for she was very close to him.

"My sister Rachel and I look very similar, being sisters and all," Bathsheba said with a sigh, "and she just may have found a way to follow me down here. She does that sometimes." Into the surprised and wary silence following what she said, she simpered shamelessly at Officer Welson. "Les sœurs peuvent être si irritantes, n'est pas?" she asked huskily.

Mauri almost groaned aloud. Besides that Bathsheba was behaving ridiculously, Mauri had taken enough French in high school to know that Bathsheba was butchering the language. She cringed inwardly for her triple–great aunt. What could the woman be about?

Officer Welson at first attempted to hide his appalled reaction, but he was soon trying to edge away from her in the crowded room. "I'll thank you to keep a decent distance," he flashed angrily, "and to keep all of what you say in English."

Bathsheba giggled. "Well, I'll try, Officer. But I declare, somehow my French just keeps popping out whenever I'm with you." And she grinned and batted her eyes at him shamelessly.

The other lawman snickered. "Guess I understand now why you were so keen to investigate this here case, Tom," he said to Officer Welson.

Officer Welson reddened and cleared his throat uncomfortably. He jabbed his pen at a fresh page in his small black notebook.

"What's your sister's full name?" he asked Bathsheba. "And no French now," he warned her.

Bathsheba put on a subdued expression and gave his sister Rachel's full name.

'Careful,' Mauri warned Bathsheba mentally. 'Officer Welson may not be brilliant, but if he catches you in a lie he'll be like a terrier that won't let go.' And as if Bathsheba heard Mauri's warning, she turned to her and blinked slowly with a serene smile. 'I know what I'm doing,' the smile seemed to say. 'It'll be your funeral,' was Mauri's mental retort, with an outward shrug of her shoulders.

"Address," Officer Welson said. "Your sister's address."

Bathsheba tilted her head way over to one side, and put a forefinger coquettishly on one cheek. "Oh," she said, almost purring, "Rachel hasn't had an address for . . . years. That is, I wouldn't know what it is if she's had one. We haven't been on, ah, speaking terms since she, well, since she stole my beau." The pretense in Bathsheba's voice dropped away and tears glistened in her eyes. "Many years ago," she finished in a thin weepy voice with her head demurely down. "La cruauté des sœurs — oh, I'm sorry, er, Officer — er, Tom. I do keep forgetting that you are particular about my not using the language of *love*." She had edged closer to Officer Welson's side again, and her left elbow was bumping his pen arm.

Officer Welson rolled his eyes, sweating.

"Well, if you don't know where she lives," he asked doggedly, "then why do you think she'd follow —"

But Officer Burns was already striding toward the door. "Nip it, Tom," he barked. Then, "C'mon, Clarence. I'll take you back. I got better things to do than this all." Clarence followed him out.

Officer Welson glared at his fellow officer's back. He obviously wasn't satisfied. He flipped through his notebook, in an effort to rally his concentration. But six pairs of eyes were staring at him fixedly, and they had their effect. He snapped his notebook shut and, with a parting glare at Bathsheba, beat a retreat.

"Au revoir, Monsieur. Jusqu'à ce que nous nous revoyions." Bathsheba cooed after him in that strange husky voice she used when speaking French. Mauri winced.

Pops went further than that. He spoke into the silence of the room as car doors slammed and tires crunched on the gravel outside.

"You might have enough gumption to burn a wet mule, womun," he said, "but it just ain't smart to get that man's tail up."

"Pops," Mauri asked, "do you really believe all this? That Bathsheba and Zekial have been zapped through time from 1859 to now?"

"Well, they here, ain't they, girl?" Pops replied, as if to a slow child.

"But —"

"You belief in these here molecules?"

"Ah, molecules?"

"Molecules," Pops pronounced deliberately. "Atoms. See here, when the nu'clar plant be built across the river, I do consider'ble study o' them speedin' molecules. I do study 'em, 'cause seem to be these're the same molecules that kill off all them Jap'nese city folk in '45."

Pop's head swiveled around to Prentis.

"You recollect how many Jap'nese folk die from them molecules?" he asked.

Prentis shook his head, but Mauri answered for him. "About 215,000."

Bathsheba gasped. "215,000 people! Was it, was it an epidemic?" she asked.

"It was a bomb," Mauri answered her when Pops did not speak. "Two bombs actually, to end a world war."

"A world war . . .," Bathsheba repeated faintly. Then, "What's a, a bomb?"

"An explosive device. Like gun powder, dynamite. Only these bombs were many, many times more powerful."

"Gracious Lord," Bathsheba breathed out. "Why, 215,000, killed by two bombs? 215,000, that's about 100,000 more than the entire population of New Orleans — our biggest southern city!"

"Whole lot o' folk," Pops commented. "Whole lot. An' all from these here molecules, these here lectrons buzzin' 'round the neutrons.

"Now, nobody done show me any o' these molecules. They done put the sketchins in the paper, and Prentis here have sketched me out

64

some more for' my studyin' o' them. But they say that all these here molecules be too small fo' to see. Way too small. But I 'spect everybody belief the results o' them there molecules. They sure belief what they do, even if none o' us ever be seein' them.

"An' now here be this womun and Zekial. An' as soon as I be hearin' Zekial's way o' talk — he talk like my grandmother did, back in the early 1900s, an' where you gonna get a boy talk like that these days? An' what he sayin', an' who he talkin' about . . . I *know* he ain't from this part of this here century. So he the result o' somethin' that I can't see, but he be here, an' I belief him."

Mauri looked from face to face. Pop and Prentis, unrevealing. Stan and Bathsheba, contemplative. Zekial, totally bewildered.

"Molecules and such are explained by physics," Mauri maintained. "Science. There's a logic to it, once you know the rules. Even what we can't see follows principles, rules of matter.

"But what law of physics or, or of biology or anything else would explain these two . . . time travelers? They're mortal, physical beings who . . . who — Zekial, tell me again about your dream. The dream that you said brought you into this century."

Zekial looked up at Mauri and blinked when she spoke his name. "Dream?" he asked softly. Then, "Dream," he stated, and frowned with thought. He didn't say anything else for a while. He sat on the bed, lost in unruly, perplexing musings. He held his body stiffly, his hands opening and closing from an inner tension, his legs sometimes shuffling back and forth clumsily. His head lolled and then jerked up, several times, with no coordination to his other movements. Suddenly his body tremored, like a jolt had run through it, and then it relaxed into a boneless slump. His expression settled into a dazed, far off look and a hum gurgled unevenly in his throat.

"Zek'l! Zek'l!" he suddenly hissed urgently, his voice at an unnaturally high pitch. "I been tryin' an' tryin' — what dis hea dream yu go in git yo'sef into, boy?" he jabbered, nearly incoherent. "Yu come on out, yu come on back now, y'harkin' me boy? Everbody be lookin' for' yu and dat Missy Theba. Dey done tear up all de cabins, an' dey be screamin' at us all eber which a way. Cursin' an' — an' dey got de houns' out from all 'roun. An' all 'o dem be lookin' so hard at us, an' — Zek'l yu know what dey gwyne do nex. Dey's gwyne be whippin us! Dey's gwyne be whippin' us til one o' us say whea yu is,

65

what yu done. So I callin' yu honey chile. Yu come back now Zek'll! Yu jus got to git on ba– —"

Zekial lurched up into the air and yelled, but then the weight of his body carried him heavily to the floor. He lay there, writhing and shuddering, knees raising up one after the other, like he was trying to run somewhere. Then he scrambled up and hugged himself, panting and moaning, rocking forward and back.

Bathsheba went over and planted herself in front of him, peering sharply into his face. Zekial looked back at her face sleepily at first, and then his eyes flew open and he stared. "Missus! Missus!" he gurgled in a strange falsetto.

Bathsheba seized Zekial's shoulders and kept her eyes locked with his. "I don't think we can come back, Bette," she said into his eyes, and Zekial drew back convulsively, as if he was terrified.

"Ghosties!" he whined through clenched teeth. "Ghosties!"

"Just listen to me, Bette," Bathsheba insisted. "Too much has happened. I don't think we can come back."

Zekial shook his head slowly while staring wildly at Bathsheba's face.

"Tell them," Bathsheba said distinctly, "tell them that you saw me fall into the river, and that Zekial went, went in after me. They won't believe you. They'll say that Zekial pushed me in and ran away. But tell them that anyway.

"And tell, tell them," she said, choking a little, "tell them that I called out for Douglas before I got swept away. They, they'll . . . that'll sound convincing. Remember that. I called out for my Douglas."

Zekial's eyes closed and his body gave out. He flopped down sideways, unconscious. After a few moments of surprise Stan and Prentis went to Zekial and lifted him onto the bed.

"Should we call a doctor, Pops?" Prentis asked his grandfather.

"Nope," Pops replied unperturbed, a thin knowing smile on his mask–like face. "No need. He'll sleep it off fine now. Sleep it off fine."

Chapter 7

The next day dawned crisp and clear, a bright Sunday morning at the end of October. Mauri lay still when she woke, wondering if yesterday had all been a wild dream, and hoping that when she rolled over she was not going to find her triple–great aunt in the other bed.

She didn't.

But the bedding was strewn around and there was a note on the dresser. "I have gone for an airing," the note said in an elaborate, spiky script. Mauri muttered to herself as she dropped back into her bed and pulled up the covers.

Plans were going to be made today for settling the time orphans into the latter part of the twentieth century. Prentis's parents were expected back from a weekend wedding in the afternoon, but Prentis and his grandfather had already indicated that they would "See to Zekial," as Pops put it.

So Zekial had fallen into the hands of receptive relatives. But even if he hadn't — even if Zekial hadn't been distantly related to Prentis's family — Mauri sensed that they would have been willing to help him anyway.

Not so with Bathsheba. Stan had pointedly interested himself in Zekial's welfare rather than Bathsheba's, and Mauri reluctantly found herself alone as Bathsheba's temporary guardian. She took on the role unwillingly, from a queer sense of family duty. And without that thin strand of kinship, she would have followed her inclination to have nothing further to do with Bathsheba.

Mauri didn't like Bathsheba. Even allowing for some resilience and some verve on Bathsheba's part, Mauri still didn't like the way the girl assumed a bossy tone whenever she seemed to get comfortable with her surroundings. And her flirtatious tack with Officer Welson was not only needlessly dumb, it was demeaning. Short term, it looked like it had worked to get Officer Welson out of their hair, but it might still land them all in some trouble with the law.

67

Well, at least their contact with Bathsheba might be mercifully short. Mauri grunted into her pillow. Bathsheba had soon made it clear that all she wanted from Mauri and Stan was some help in finding her white kin.

"We'll try to help you," Mauri had snapped, "but don't be so sure that any of them will want to know you."

"I only meant —"

"Just don't forget that Stan and I are as much your kin as any of them will ever be."

Mauri had gotten her father's family tree out and they had poured over its entries. But the current generation was sketchy. At least twenty years had passed since her father's marriage had severed contact with his family.

"It seems to me that the most promising lines," Bathsheba had commented after studying the tree, "are the children and grandchildren of your grandfather's brother and sister."

"We'll have to ask Prentis and Pops about them in the morning," Mauri had yawned.

And now it was morning, still pretty early. Mauri got up and knocked softly at Number 17. All was quiet inside, so she headed up to the motel office with her father's binder. There she found that she was actually the last one up.

"Zekial woke me up at exactly four–oh–two this morning," Stan told her with wry glumness.

Prentis and Stan had been explaining to Zekial about Reverend Martin Luther King.

"Hey, Sis," Stan soon broke off, "we're all starving. Let's you and me go get everybody something to eat."

They got some directions from Prentis for a place on the highway that would be open.

"So you've been telling Zekial about our history," Mauri commented on the way to the car.

"Yeah. We've been telling him mostly the history book stuff, and Prentis has been rounding it out with local stories. Now and then I put in something that I know firsthand."

"How much of it do you think he's absorbing?"

"Well, some. Some. But . . . knowing is one thing, and really understanding it is something else, Sis. It's going to be hard for Zekial not to think like a slave."

"That's because he was one less than twenty–four hours ago. It'll take time."

"Yeah. But I'm wondering if that'll ever be enough. Being a slave is like, real ingrained in him."

They talked about Zekial for the rest of the way to the food place on the highway. When they got back into the car with their take out, Mauri broached the subject of Bathsheba.

"What are we going to do about her, Stan?"

"Ah, what do you mean 'we', Sis?"

"Stan, I'm going to need some help with this. What you're doing to help Zekial is great and all, but Bathsheba's sort of our problem. She's our relative."

"Please don't remind me."

"You know how unlikely it is that any of her white kin will take her in."

"Oh, I dunno. Maybe one of them has a business and can give her a job. Anyway, she's white. She can read and write. She'll do alright once she gets a job."

"She's got no birth certificate — none that anybody would believe anyway — so she can't get a social security number. She's got no higher education worth mentioning, and her French accent is just terrible."

"That bad?"

"Probably not worth salvaging. And she's got no job history. If she's lucky enough to get a job, it'll be minimum wage — not enough to support herself, even around here."

Stan was silent for a while. "Think anybody'd marry her?" he then asked.

Mauri snorted. "Well, there's no accounting for people's taste, but I wouldn't count on that particular solution if I were you."

"Yeah, I guess not. And if anybody did show that kind of interest in her, I bet she'd queer it on purpose."

"Oh? What makes you say that?"

"Ah, I dunno. Just a guess. Maybe it was the way she played Officer Welson — you know, flirting with him and all. She did it to

69

throw him off his little 'investigation', and I'm sure that even Officer Welson realizes it. But she was mocking him too, you know? Like maybe she hated him much more that his nosiness warranted."

Bathsheba still hadn't returned from her "airing" when Mauri and Stan got back to the motel.

During the meal in the office Zekial kept pausing and listening. Finally Stan asked him what was the matter.

Zekial started eating again with a nervous smile. "I be expectin' t' hear de Missus callin' me to git t' some work or t'other," Zekial said. "'Fetch mo' wood from de sheds.' 'Load up de wagons from de flat dat jus' tie up.' 'Take ol' Missus Preston across on de ferry.' 'Fetch some mo' barrels o' oil.' All de time, an' always when I jus' be sittin' down t' eat or t' res'.

"But here I be, at dis here feast." He shook his head over his buttery grits and golden hash browns. "An' it jus' not seemin' real somehow. I git t' tink I be dreamin', an' dat Missus gwyne t' holler me onto somethin' or t'other any time now."

"You do a lot of day dreaming, Zekial?" Stan asked.

"All de time, Stannie. All de time. I 'scape dat way. 'Scape dat way." He gingerly lifted his styrofoam coffee cup and his nostrils flared over the fragrant black liquid. "Mmmm," he sniffed pleasurably, "But dis . . . dis all's jus' heaben. Dis be betterin' dreamin'."

After the meal Mauri showed Prentis the family tree and asked if he thought any of Bathsheba's relatives were at all likely to help her out. Prentis studied the family tree gravely.

"This isn't complete."

"There's been no contact for the last twenty years or so. Would you, um, mind giving me some of the missing details?"

But Prentis shook his head. "I'd rather not," he said.

"Oh?"

"See, I wouldn't pursue this idea, if I were you."

"You don't think they'd help her?"

"They won't even believe who she is to them. How could they?"

"Well, I was going to let her handle that part of it. She seems fairly, ah, resourceful."

Prentis snorted and shook his head. "Better let that alone," he advised. "Let the sleeping dog lie." Then he joined Stan in trying to explain Kwanzaa to Zekial.

"I'll be sure to pass on your advice to Bathsheba," Mauri said to his back. He knew something but wasn't telling, and it irritated her.

The morning advanced and Bathsheba still didn't return. At about eleven o'clock, Mauri decided to go out and look for her.

"She's probably gone out to the old Spit, where you were last night," Prentis commented.

"But that's at least seven miles from here."

Stan shrugged and said, "It's not so bad. I walked it yesterday easily."

"But there's nothing there but, but a chain link fence and kudzu."

Stan shrugged again. "Well, if she's not in Officer Welson's jail by now, where else would she be?"

"Somewhere . . . anywhere but there," Mauri replied. But then she decided that the old landing might be the best place to start looking after all. So she took some of the breakfast for Bathsheba and headed for the car. "Call in the marines if I'm not back in two hours," she said over her shoulder.

"Check," said Stan as the spring door slammed behind her.

* * *

Mauri slipped under the fence and fought her way through the undergrowth toward the old landing. In the bright sunlight the place had a surreal appearance: Mauri tried to imagine a bustling plantation in place of the scraggly, kudzu–choked brush and woods. If Bathsheba was here, what would she be making of this abandoned landscape?

Mauri found Bathsheba at the river fence by the landing, staring through the weave of chain link at the river trudging by.

"I've brought you some breakfast," Mauri told her gruffly, feeling unreasonably like a slave serving her mistress, instead of someone helping out a destitute relative. She found herself secretly glad that the food and the coffee were stark cold.

"Why, thank you very kindly," Bathsheba said vaguely. "I was just starting to get hungry."

71

They sat down on a jumble of rocks nearby. Bathsheba didn't seem to notice that the food was stiff and lumpy.

"Where we're sitting is — was — the front corner of the main warehouse," she mused. "There were four of them, two on each side of the landing. Bathsheba looked around dully. "The whole place looks so different now," she said wistfully.

Mauri shrugged with deliberateness. "Now it's probably more like it was before it was ever cleared and farmed," she commented.

Bathsheba nodded slowly. "All that hard work to clear this land. My great grandparents started it, but it was my father's parents who made it what it . . . was. They were cousins, and their marriage combined two adjoining farms. My grandfather added to it until it was nineteen hundred acres and the ferry."

"And how many slaves?" Mauri asked.

Bathsheba looked at her and then looked away. "About two hundred, as of 1859," she answered evenly.

"It's a shame that the slaves had no share in all the wealth that was built up," Mauri commented dryly.

"Most of them aren't — weren't — very . . . ah . . . intelligent." Bathsheba replied complacently.

"Do you really believe that?!" Mauri shot back. "Well, history has proved you wrong, sister. As a group, African Americans aren't any dumber or smarter than anybody else. It's more a matter of opportunity and, and expectations."

"Indeed," Bathsheba commented frostily.

Mauri stood up. "We'd better go, er, Theba. We've got to make some plans, and this just doesn't seem to be a good place for doing that."

They got all the way to the hole under the fence in a stormy silence. But it's hard to twist through a washout with someone and come out on the other side with as much pride and reserve as you went into it with. When Theba soon afterward gave a conciliatory warning for a ground hole in Mauri's path, Mauri eased out of her ill feelings somewhat.

"Prentis thinks it's a bad idea for you to try to contact any white kin around here," Mauri stated baldly.

"In my day no one would think of going calling without an introduction."

"Nowadays things aren't usually quite so formal. But they'd want to know why you're seeking their, ah, friendship."

Bathsheba sighed and nodded. "Yes, that's the trouble."

When they were in the car and on their way back toward Mirard, Bathsheba spoke. "I'm wondering if you would do me a kindness. There's one more thing I'd like to see before I turn my full attention to the present. And the future."

"Shoot."

"Ah, pardon?"

"I mean, go ahead. Tell me where you want to go."

Bathsheba guided Mauri into Mirard and a few streets beyond what was apparently its main intersection.

"This is bewildering," Bathsheba said edgily, peering through the windshield. "Everything is so — oh! Turn off to the left here!"

Mauri missed the turn but pulled into a parking lot and backtracked. A small church was at the end of the short street that Bathsheba had chosen, and cars lined both sides of the street and filled a parking lot beside the church. Mauri parked in the first gap she could find along the street.

Bathsheba then led her through the parking lot to a cemetery behind the church. A hearty swell of singing voices came from inside the church as Bathsheba searched among the gravestones. Mauri glanced at her watch. It was almost 12:30; the singing was probably the closing hymn, and that meant that the church would probably be emptying soon.

"This is stupid, Theba," Mauri whispered irritably. She felt that she had enough to worry about without enduring the righteous — or worse — stares of a white presbyterian congregation. "Let's leave before —"

"Here it is. Here I am," Bathsheba announced, looking down at an old marker.

Still hoping to get away before the church started emptying, Mauri decided to humor Bathsheba by looking at the stone. It read:

Bathsheba Bethay Severly
Died October 29, 1859
Aged 19 Years
Suddenly in the River

And then it was too late. The back door of the church opened, and a man and an elderly woman stepped out into the cemetery. Mauri had never seen the woman before, but she immediately recognized Officer Welson, even without his uniform. She nudged Bathsheba, and both girls watched as the lawman guided the woman down the narrow cemetery paths toward them.

Chapter 8

"Who are those people, Tommie?" they heard the old woman ask querulously.

"They're two of the strangers that I was telling you about," Officer Tom Welson replied.

"One of them is a black. And that white girl, she's the one who stole your great aunt's name?"

"Looks that way, Grandmama. Looks that way."

Welson and his grandmother reached the gravestone. He and Bathsheba exchanged icy stares, and then Welson read the tombstone as if to check that it hadn't changed. He nodded.

"Bathsheba is a real uncommon name," he stated. "Real uncommon. And my grandmother here reminded me this morning that we had an ancestor with that name. After that we come to realize that the name you gave me last night matches the one on this grave stone exactly."

"I am Mrs. Welson," the old woman spoke stiffly and harshly to Bathsheba. "And the Bathsheba in this grave was my great aunt, as she is my grandson's here. And what we want to know is, why are you using her name? Who are you, and what are you doing here with her name?"

Bathsheba dallied before answering. She looked beyond Mrs. Welson to the back of the church. "This isn't the church building that was here in my day," she stated. "Then it was red brick with a much smaller spire.

The old woman's eyes were in a cold fury now. "Who are you? Just exactly who are you?" she repeated angrily.

Bathsheba put her hand on her grave marker. "The person in this grave is not Bathsheba Bethay Severly. Some poor soul must have been drowned in the storm and washed up downriver sometime later, and they must have thought it was me."

"Tom!" exclaimed Mrs. Welson. "This girl is plumb crazy!"

"Hear me out," Bathsheba retorted. "It won't take long."

Bathsheba then described how she and Zekial had come into the 1990s from 1859. While she spoke the church was emptying. A few people stopped to stare at them on the way to their cars, but none came over: apparently the Welsons' presence reassured them to the point of disinclination. 'They'll all be wanting to get home to their dinners,' Mauri thought, 'or maybe the Welsons aren't all that popular around here.'

"And then we slipped under the fence and walked to — I made that up about my sister Rachel being out on the back roads, of course. She stayed back in 1859 and married my beau, Judge Douglas Pritchard — I believe that'd be your husband's grandfather, Mrs. Welson.

No one spoke when Bathsheba finished. Tom Welson scratched his ear with his eyebrows high, but his grandmother looked like a fury.

"You insult the dignity of my family," Mrs. Welson finally spat out.

"It's quite the other way around," Bathsheba sniffed. "Judging by your son's choice of profession, it seems to me the family's prestige has fallen considerably since I was — since 1859."

"Why you lying vixen —," Mrs. Welson began.

"Grandmama, please," Tom Welson hastened to interject. "Don't let this crazy person overexcite you. She's nothing at all to us."

"Doesn't matter who she is!" Mrs. Welson hissed. "No one has the right to defile the memory of —" Mrs. Welson jabbed her forefinger at Bathsheba. "My grandson Tommie wanted to go to law school, but he took a job here instead to see to me. He's a good boy —"

Officer Tom Welson reddened and groaned.

"He's the only direct family I have left. I helped raise him, and I depend on him now."

Bathsheba gave an ugly snort. "Why, it wouldn't hurt you a bit to let him go away to school for a few years. And he could visit you — more likely he's just plain afraid to go to law school. Afraid that —"

"We seem to have gotten off the main subject," Tom Welson said testily to Bathsheba, "and it's none of your business anyway, young woman. Now, it seems to me that you and your friend here have broken a trespassing law or two —"

"I did not really expect you to believe me," Bathsheba retorted. "I would not have believed it myself except that I'm, well, I'm here. I don't have any choice in the matter. But what good would it do anybody to put me in jail?"

"Theba," Mauri spoke up, "there might be a trial, and at the trial nobody would believe you. They could have you, um, committed to a mental hospital as, as an insane person."

"Do you mean an, an asylum for the mentally imbalanced?" Bathsheba asked, and Mauri nodded.

A thin triumphant smile creased Mrs. Welson's face, and Bathsheba visibly paled. "Then, then what would happen to me?" she whispered, clearly frightened by this prospect.

"Well, I'm not sure," Mauri replied. "But I don't think it would be as bleak as it might have been back in the 1850s. I suppose that after they realize that you're, um, harmless, they'd try to rehabilitate you. You'd live in a halfway house — a supervised place outside of the hospital, and you'd be given a job of some kind."

Bathsheba shook her head dazedly and began to twist her ring. "Well," she sighed, breathless. "Well. That wouldn't be my first choice for the future. I do admit that. I do."

"Tommie!" Mrs. Welson exclaimed, pointing at Bathsheba's hand. "That girl is a thief! She is wearing my ring!"

Bathsheba stepped back and shook her head vehemently. "Maybe Rachel's ring has been passed down to you," she said. "We both had a ring like this. Papa brought them to us all the way from Philadelphia. They are — were — the same, except for our initials inside. That way we could always tell them apart. This one is not yours. It's mine."

Mrs. Welson sputtered and put out her hand imperiously for the ring, but Bathsheba shook her head. "This ring and the dress I came here in are all I've got to prove who I am," she maintained. "I won't give it over to anyone I don't trust. And I certainly don't trust you."

But she slipped the ring off her finger and handed it to Mauri. "Please read them the initials inside the ring, Mauri."

"B.B.S.," Mauri read, and handed the ring back to Bathsheba.

There was an awkward silence.

"If Officer Welson wishes to arrest me, then so be it," Bathsheba said nervously.

Officer Welson cleared his throat. "Just hold your ring out, please, so that I can see the initials."

"I give you my word," he added, "that I won't take the ring from you."

Bathsheba eyed him carefully and then did as he asked.

"She's right about the initials, Grandmother," he admitted, blinking. "And, and I don't believe that this one looks as worn as yours is."

Bathsheba nodded. "They were only given to us last winter — that is, in the winter of 1859."

But Mrs. Welson's face was hostile, disbelieving. "Tom, she's stolen that ring from somewhere, and the dress she talks of. Depend upon it! Just like she's stolen our poor ancestor's name. Don't let this girl go and make a big fool of you!" she warned. "What she's saying is just impossible."

Officer Welson nodded absently. His eyes were fixed on the ring, now back on Bathsheba's finger.

"Either way, it's all very farfetched, highly farfetched," he muttered uneasily. He shook his head heavily, staring from one girl to the other. Then he cleared his throat and squared his shoulders. "I'm going to take my grandmother home now," he told Mauri and Bathsheba, "and then I'll come by the motel to question you further. Ms. Severly, can I depend upon your being there when I arrive at, say, two o'clock?"

"You have my word," Bathsheba replied haughtily.

Mauri found it very hard to read Officer Tom Welson and Bathsheba at that moment. Was he really expecting Bathsheba to be at the motel when he arrived, or was he giving her an opportunity to escape? And did Bathsheba really intend to keep her word, or was she going to try to hide as soon as this lawman was out of sight?

Officer Welson escorted his grandmother out of the cemetery. Bathsheba deliberately dawdled among the stones, reading them here and there. She found her father's, and Rachel's and her beau's.

"What are you going to do?" Mauri asked her as soon as Officer Welson and his grandmother were out of earshot.

78

"I don't know," Bathsheba replied softly. "I don't know. But I am thinking on it."

"Let's get back to the motel," said Mauri, shivering, "Prentis may have some ideas."

When they arrived back at the motel they found everyone in the motel office. Prentis's parents had returned and Mauri and Bathsheba were quickly introduced. Mrs. McBride was a very capable looking woman with intelligent eyes. Her husband moved slowly and had difficulty breathing. His wife explained that he had a heart ailment.

When Mauri told everyone about Officer Welson's proposed "visit", Mrs. McBride asked her to repeat word for word what Officer Welson had said. She listened intently and nodded. "This here white girl should leave," she stated flatly. "Get her out of the county. And you youngins — indicating Mauri and Stan — "had better get good and gone with her."

"But I gave my word, ma'am," Bathsheba asserted obstinately.

"Don't matter none," Mrs. McBride came right back at her. "I've known Tommy Welson since he was in diapers. One o' my aunties used to do his family's wash afore his father die in 'Nam an' his ma go off her head. An' I tell you, girlie, all he wants is for you t'git outta his part of this here county."

Bathsheba licked her lips. "What about Zekial?" she asked Mrs. McBride.

"Never you mind 'bout Zekial," Mrs. McBride replied. "We'll see to Zekial."

"Alright," agreed Bathsheba, a little breathlessly. "Alright." She turned to Mauri and Stan. "We'd better go — I mean, if you wouldn't mind driving me somewhere . . . away from here."

"Wait," Mauri spoke up. "That sheriff deputy's got the registration and license number of my rental car. And he's got full identification on both Stan and me."

Mrs. McBride turned her heavy lidded eyes on Mauri, and Mauri understood why Bathsheba had agreed with the woman so readily. She was Pops, between forty and fifty years younger. A deep outrage lodged in her eyes, resident with a wary resignation.

"You jus' do as I tell you, girl," Mrs. McBride told Mauri.

Mauri and Stan packed their things and Bathsheba folded her sodden dress and cape into a plastic bag, and in fifteen minutes they were back in the motel office. Bathsheba asked Mrs. McBride for an envelope, and Mauri saw Bathsheba put her ring and a note she'd written to Officer Welson into it. Then she handed it back to Mrs. McBride, along with the bag with her dress and cape in it.

Prentis left with Zekial in his car, and soon Mauri, Stan and Bathsheba were also pulling out of the motel lot. Mr. and Mrs. McBride were left to face Officer Welson when he arrived, which was exactly the way they wanted it.

Mauri picked up the interstate at Augusta and arrived at the Atlanta airport three hours later. They stopped only once, to buy a suitcase for Bathsheba and some things to put in it. While Bathsheba stared wide–eyed at the commerce in a huge Walmart's receding aisles, Mauri and Stan grabbed the cheapest fill they could find, which happened to be a combination of paper towels, toilet paper and some clearance clothing.

At the airport Mauri bought three tickets for the next flight to New York. After eating sandwiches they sat near a large plate glass window so that Bathsheba could see the planes taking off and landing. Apart from Stan's aerodynamic explanations, there was little talk among them.

Not long before their flight boarded, Mauri phoned the McBrides.

"Come and gone," Mr. McBride drawled about Officer Welson's visit. "No tellin' what he might do, sugar, but I wouldn't worry about him none. You jus' keep that white girl outta this county, thas all." Mauri promised him that she would try, and Mr. McBride rung off with a dry chuckle before Mauri could thank him for his family's advice and help.

"So this thing is really going to go up into the air . . ." Bathsheba said nervously when they got to their adjoining seats on the plane. Mauri assured her that it would. "Very powerful engines," Mauri whispered. "Forces air across the wings. Lifts right up." Bathsheba nodded, but she gulped so audibly that people across the aisle glanced over.

The plane lumbered out to its appointed runway and lined up ponderously for its takeoff. Then it put on speed, its engines whining higher and higher until the vibrations changed subtly and the sense of being off the ground came. They were airborne, headed away from the family past — except for one exceedingly tense and awkward chunk of it.

Overall Bathsheba managed the plane's takeoff and ascent with remarkable control. Several times she tried to turn the ring that was no longer on her finger, and her breath came in short ragged gasps whenever her glance strayed to the windows. But she kept a grip on her nerves, her fluster.

She clutched the armrests rigidly when the plane dropped slightly and shuddered in some turbulence, and she drew breath and held it with her eyes shut tight. The people across the aisle watched surreptitiously, fascinated by this particular phobic flyer. Mauri and Stan waited for her release of breath, and when it did eventually come, slowly and raggedly, the people across the aisle gave her a splatter of applause.

"You're doin' okay kid," Stan told her, "for a country girl."

"The only thing," Bathsheba wheezed back, immediately recapturing the flagging interest from across the aisle, "that keeps me from runnin' mad through the walkways of this . . . this place is, is seein' how everybody *else* in here is actin' just so confoundly n–, n–, normal!"

"Then open your eyes and keep watching them," Stan advised reasonably, "It'll take your mind off the fact that you're oh, about 30,000 feet up in the —"

A gurgle rattling in Bathsheba's throat stopped Stan midsentence.

"Oh. Sorry about the thirty thou– —"

"It's alright," Bathsheba squeaked. "Just — please don't mention it again." It was a long time before her grasp on the armrest lessened.

Mauri marked the time that it took for Bathsheba's hands to relax, and she marked that Bathsheba, without being too obvious, was following Stan's advice. She watched the people across the aisle about as surreptitiously as they watched her, and she gazed at the steward and stewardesses whenever they trekked up and down the aisles.

Bathsheba started sniffling about an hour into the flight. And then sneezing.

"I do believe I have an indisposition in my nose and head," she said with the unmistakable resonance of stopped–up sinuses.

"You'll probably catch quite a few colds this winter," Stan commented from the other side of Mauri. "There are probably a lot of viruses that you haven't been exposed to."

"Er, viruses?" Bathsheba honked, and Stan launched into a description of T cells and antibodies. It passed the time, and helped to distract Bathsheba from the fact that she was moving through the air at approximately 30,000 feet.

They'd been doing that sort of thing all afternoon with Bathsheba: acclimatizing her to the latter part of the 20th century on a haphazard, take–what–comes basis. Fast–forwarding Bathsheba over one hundred and forty years in a headlong embrace with science and technology, Mauri wondered several times about how Zekial was faring, on his second day in what was to him a strange new world.

Some of it had been easy and kind of fun, like when Stan told Bathsheba about the significance of the name brands emblazoned across things like T–shirts and the waist bands of underwear in the big Walmart store.

But other parts had been unexpectedly difficult. How do you adequately explain the anonymity of interstate automobile travel to someone used to a horse–drawn buggy on dirt roads? Or the scale of a nationwide — even worldwide — system for a plastic card that buys everything from gas to food to ugly boxy suitcases and airline tickets?

The further north they flew, the more subdued Bathsheba became. It might have been the effect of her worsening head congestion, or the pitch blackness outside the plane. She barely registered the plane's landing at LaGuardia, and had to be roused out of a daze to get off the plane.

In the terminal Mauri called her mother to let her know that she and Stan would be arriving at the house in about forty–five minutes. At first her mother sounded delighted to hear that Mauri was coming in with Stan. Then she sounded puzzled.

"I thought that you and Stan were going to be in Georgia for several more days."

"We were."

"And I thought that you were going to fly straight back to Pittsburgh, Mauri."

"I was."

Pause. Then, "What's wrong, Mauri?" her mother asked. "Are you two okay?"

"Mom, we're fine. We're just fine. Georgia's a lovely place, though it was, ah, swampier than I expected. I only had to rescue Stan from a couple of quicksand bogs, and he only had to snatch me from the jaws of a few vicious alligators, just in the nicks of time. They were big, Ma, those gators were big. And their teeth — they had wicked, wicked teeth, Ma."

"Oh, Mauri. You and your stor– — you two weren't really anywhere near a swamp . . . were you?"

"Well, actually," Mauri drew a deep breath. "You're right. No quicksand. No gators. However, we are bringing someone home with us."

"Someone?"

"Yes."

"Mauri, what are you hiding from me?"

"It's kinda hard to explain over the phone. We'll tell you all about it when we all get there."

"I'm not going to like this, am I, Mauri?"

"Probably not. I don't like it much either, actually. Neither does Stan."

"Then why —"

"But, hey, we're all in one piece. No limbs missing. No blood lost — though I did skin a knuckle in a mud puddle. And we haven't been arrested for anything. Not yet anyway. That's something."

The line was silent.

"Are you still there, Ma?" Mauri asked.

"Girl, you just get yourself here as soon as you can with Stan and, ah, whoever else."

"Yes'm," Mauri replied, and hung up.

* * *

When Mauri called her office at noon the next day to check for messages, the phone rang and rang. When someone finally answered, it wasn't one of the regular receptionists. The voice was tentative, odd–sounding.

"This is Mauri Bale. I'm down for personal days through Wednesday, and I'm calling in for messages."

"Ah, messages? Messages," the voice replied.

"Yes. Messages. You know, those funny little — um, is something wrong there?"

Silence on the other end of the line.

"Are any of the other juniors in?" Mauri then asked. She thought over who would be in. "Mark, Jerry or Lisa? Can you put me through to one of them?"

"Hold please," and the line clicked and whispered.

"Jerry here. Mauri?"

"Yeah, it's me."

"Hey! How's Georgia?"

"Short trip. Long story. But what's going on there? The woman at reception sounded, well, odd. And why isn't our ever faithful Linda answering the phone? Or Joan?"

"Mauri, Linda is one of them, and we think that Joan is too."

"Ah, one of who?"

"Well, it seems that over the weekend the firm split into two firms, Mauri."

"You're got to be kidding!"

"Wish I was, Mauri. Wish I was."

Jerry then told her about how a cadre of partners and seniors had cleared out their desks and taken files from the file room over the weekend. They left a letter taped to the firm's door, announcing the establishment of their own firm, and claiming a long list of fairly significant clients. Ah, thought Mauri, that explains the guy in the file room. It wasn't romance. It wasn't gas. Just plain old theft.

"They'll never get away with it," Mauri said.

Jerry disagreed. "There'll eventually be some sort of settlement, after a lawsuit or two is filed. But the national affiliation is only a few years old, and apparently it didn't suit a number of the partners. The sore points were things like lower profits, clients grumbling about higher fees and such."

"So what about us juniors?" Mauri asked. "What happens to us?"

"Good question, Mauri. I was just wondering about that myself. The defectors supposedly didn't tell any of us juniors in advance. But I wouldn't be surprised if some knew."

"Not me."

"Me either," Jerry admitted.

Mauri got some details about the defectors' client list, and sat thinking things over after she rung off. With nearly half of the major clients suddenly gone, there was bound to be an excess of juniors.

Mauri picked up the phone again and called the Personnel Manager at a large Manhattan accounting firm. He'd made her a job offer right out of school which she'd politely declined, wanting to move to a different city. He took her call now and when she described the unusual goings on at her Pittsburgh firm he put her on hold for a few minutes. When he got back on the line he made her a job offer. They were hiring for the tax and audit season and would be delighted to have her with them.

Mauri accepted and then called the Pittsburgh firm to announce her resignation. The personnel manager there sounded relieved, and also told her that she'd gotten a call from her counterpart at Mauri's new firm a short while ago.

"Had you been planning this, Mauri, or do you just work fast?"

"The latter, in this case. I just heard about the, ah, split from one of the other juniors."

The personnel manager sighed. "Things are not going to be normal around here for quite a while, especially for the juniors. You're smart to get out early, and I wish you well."

Mauri thanked her and rung off. She called her mother at work and told her the news. She would have the rest of the week to get her things moved back from Pittsburgh, and she was sure her landlord would not be a stickler about the lease.

"Well, frankly, I'm relieved, Mauri."

"Right," Mauri agreed, trying to sound enthusiastic. "It's a fairly good career move, and this way I'll be around to help out more with Theba."

"I know you'd rather have a place of your own, Mauri. Maybe you will, a little later."

Mauri could only shrug unhappily.

"But I'm glad that you'll be here to help out with this Theba. I really don't know what we're going to do with her."

"Do you believe it, Mom? That she's from 1859? That she's actually related to us?"

"I couldn't at first. I kept expecting you and Stan to burst out laughing at the elaborate joke that I thought you were playing on me.

But then when you all stayed so serious about it . . . well, what choice do I have really?"

The rest of the week was a blur to Mauri. Stan and Bathsheba took the train with her to Pittsburgh, and the three of them got Mauri's things into her car and returned to New York. The next Monday morning came around in a blink and Mauri stood in the foyer of her mother's house, rechecking her briefcase one last time. It was 6:30 a.m.. She would leave in a few minutes to begin the commute into Manhattan for her first day at the new firm.

Bathsheba came down from the bedroom they were sharing and sat down on the bench by the door. Mauri mumbled an apology for disturbing her rest, which Bathsheba waved away.

"Sometimes I just can't believe it," Bathsheba said while staring at Mauri's trim business suit and knee–length hemline. Still heavily congested, her voice was thick and croupy. "I mean, a girl going out and working at a man's job and all."

"S'not a man's job anymore. There's a lot more things that women can do — are expected to do."

Bathsheba sniffed — not with derision but from her congestion. She blinked heavily, her face slack. Almost like a poker face.

And Mauri suddenly remembered something from two years earlier, when she had stood in this spot and her father had sat on the bench where Bathsheba was now. Mauri had been in her last year of college then and was about to leave for an important job interview. And her father had been teasing her fluttery nerves away, his face deadpan serious, with words uncannily similar to Bathsheba's.

"Now why would they want to hire a scrawny little ol' girl for a man's job?" he had jibbed.

"Little!" she had screeched, unable to believe how high and brittle her voice was. "Scrawny!"

And he had burst out laughing, further fueling her nervy outrage. "I'll show you," she had muttered darkly at him as she flounced magnificently out the front door. It was a truly grand exit. It really was. Shame that she had to retrace her steps a few moments later to get her briefcase. Her father opened the door when she reached it and handed out the briefcase with a ribald salute.

"Go get 'em, kid," he growled, and her mother's sleepy voice floated out from behind him. "Good luck, Mauri."

86

Dad sitting on the bench. Dad leaning out of the door with the briefcase . . . for a few moments he was there again, so vivid that . . . Bathsheba had stepped out of the past — why not Dad? Why couldn't Dad — Mauri turned quickly and stared hard for him on the bench. But of course there was only Bathsheba. Sniffling groggy Bathsheba.

Startled Bathsheba. "What's the matter, Mauri?" Bathsheba asked, alarmed by Mauri's stare. "You . . . you look like you're seeing a, well, um . . . a gh–, gh–, ghost," she finished self–consciously. Then she choked on a croupy giggle and in moments both girls were in a screaming morass of hysterics. Together their discordant bleats blared into a Greek chorus of thwarted hope and expectation. Mauri cawed at the absurdity of imagining her Dad back into existence, while crying from the intense disappointment that it couldn't be. Bathsheba howled about what an absurd ghost she was, while sobbing irrationally for the loss of her beau. Sometimes she wanted to go back so badly, and slap Douglas's face, and tear all of her sister's hair out. But she could never go back.

The incongruities shattered the thin membrane between normalcy and the rushing beyond. Both girls were swept in — howling, hacking, gulping for air. Without knowing how, they knew that they shared an image of falling into a cold, rain swollen river. The flesh of their faces stung painfully from the water's impact. They could hold nothing back, except the thinnest of threads for hauling themselves back to sanity, to altered reality — the stingiest of reserves for getting back across the fluid line.

"I hope you two aren't going to carry on like this at 6:30 a.m. every Monday morning," Stan growled from the upstairs hallway.

Fresh gales of laughter greeted his solemn aspiration, but some of the spontaneity had faded. The jags were shorter and wheezier. Bathsheba's laughter quieted and Mauri's did too, but not Mauri's ragged sobs. Her mother had come downstairs; she took Mauri by the shoulders. She knew what was ailing her child. Her eyes probed Mauri's.

"Maybe you should call in sick," her mother began, "even though it's your first day."

Mauri shook her head dizzily and turned away, wiping her face and grouping for her briefcase. This time she was *not* going to forget her briefcase. Dad would never be there again with his goofy salute. So gross. So —

"I'll be — okay," she said, hiccupping. "Plenty of — time — to get a — grip dur–, dur– — on the bus and the train. Bye." She forced it up her throat and grabbed for the doorknob. Shakily, blindly.

"Knock 'em dead, kid," said Stan to her back as she crossed the threshold, and she howled in agony as she rushed down the front steps.

"Good luck, Mauri," wafted her mother's voice softly after her.

"Au revoir," Bathsheba honked.

Mauri fled from them, down the sidewalk, down the street, away to dwell among blessedly anonymous strangers for a while. This would be her pattern. Bracing to the rigors of love and grief at home. Getting some relief from it at work.

When she turned at the corner she automatically mapped her route in her mind, and the interconnecting streets became like the spindly lines of a fantastical family tree. Each dull little box made from the street grids had enough space for a birth, a marriage and a death. They were laid out and spread far beyond where she was and who she was. They went in more directions than she could ever possibly go.

And then there were the diagonals, and snaking curves, which did very strange things to the rigid little rectangles. Zekial and Bathsheba things . . . and then there would be stories, lots of stories interconnecting the boxes, overlapping the boxes. True stories, impossible stories, half made up, half true stories.

But stories only tormented Mauri now. They crowded her off the sidewalk, and tottered her along the lines of the horrid little boxes. Coffins, not boxes. Falling out of one strange story into another. Falling from one coffin into another.

And then Mauri ran the grid. Just ran. Ran for the bus. Ran to get away from her grief.

Part 2 — Bathsheba's Part

Chapter 9

After Mauri left for work Bathsheba returned to the bedroom that they were sharing. She took up just a small part of the room: the rollout bed and the contents of a drawer in the bureau were hers, along with some shirts on hangers in the closet. Mauri's move back from Pittsburgh had made a much bigger impact upon the room than Bathsheba had. Boxes and displaced clothing dominated the space.

Bathsheba edged past a haphazard line of boxes and curled up in the sheets and blankets on her bed. Irregular pings and tickings sounded along the baseboard, heralding a gush of heat, and for the millionth time since her . . . drowning, Bathsheba marveled at the utter commonness that luxury had achieved in the world. Mauri had assured her over and over again that her family was not rich — only reasonably comfortable. And yet this family lived in such excessive comfort — much more than the Montgomery's, the richest planter family that Bathsheba knew.

When Bathsheba went to Pittsburgh with Mauri and Stan to help with Mauri's move, she saw block after block of houses similar to the one that she was in now. Driving out of Queens they had quickly exchanged neighborhoods for ribbons of roadway. But in Pittsburgh she had seen close up many houses, strewn thickly over the city's many hills. It made a deep impression upon her, much more so than the huge vertical buildings in New York's and Pittsburgh's downtowns. She began to comprehend the magnitude of the countryside's wealth. There were vast numbers of very comfortable people in this country now, including many — as Mauri was fond of pointing out — whose ancestors had come to it as African slaves.

Caught up in the work of the move, and perhaps because her head was stopped up most of that week, Bathsheba didn't give much thought to the incongruity of it all during the days, but at night it was difficult for her to settle with the bizarre strangeness of what common life had become. And the profusion of silly goods she had

89

seen in the stores — the excess of it all struck her as . . . indecent. It seemed far too much of plenty somehow.

People now had more than was good for them, she thought. Worse, Mauri had told her that everyone threw away much of what they had when it either broke or they grew tired of it. Bathsheba had great difficulty absorbing this. She just couldn't imagine where all of that refuse would go, where it would all be put.

And then there was the matter of the way that the descendants of the former slaves lived now. The worst fears of her people had come to be, but everybody now acted as if it was so ordinary.

Bathsheba heard Stan's door open and she traced his passage down the hall to the bathroom. Stan had been barely more than distantly polite to her, but even so she felt admiring of him. He tried to explain things to her whenever he realized that something had confused her, and his explanations were lucid and informed. And several times he had made her feel less strange by one of this 'attitudes' — joking her through something that shocked or unnerved her.

But by now he was showing a definite inclination to avoid or ignore her. He'd helped give her some grounding but he was busy with his studies and his friends. She understood. He wanted no continuing role in her acclimatization.

The sound of the shower running came faintly through the walls, and the thought of Stan undressed in the shower stall came unbidden to her mind. Water smattering his chest and arms and — she got up suddenly and busied herself with making her bed and putting away some of the clothes. She climbed over some boxes to open a window, for the heat felt stifling to her. Much of the clothing had been pulled out of the boxes to help outfit her — jeans and blouses and sweaters and t shirts and — there was so much of it. Bathsheba concentrated on folding the clothing, forcing her thoughts away from Stan and toward the impersonality of excess plentitude. She knew that she would stay in here until Stan left for his classes. She knew he preferred it that way, and she did now too, because she was afraid that she might inadvertently reveal some of the . . . confusion . . . that she was feeling about him.

* * *

90

Soon after Bathsheba's mother had died, Aunt Mary arrived to run the house. This spinster aunt came with firm ideas of how to run her bereaved brother's household, having assessed its strengths and weaknesses over many past visits. She immediately picked her younger niece Bathsheba to be her constant assistant. She had long thought that there was untapped promise in the fifteen year old girl.

Bathsheba readily accepted the duties and their considerable impingement upon her leisure, in exchange for her aunt's higher regard and friendship. She did not have Rachel's ability to ignore her aunt's unspoken pleas for assistance, or to be deaf to her aunt's unending complaints about the servants. And she lacked Rachel's talent for always being elsewhere when a woman of the house was needed for some unpleasant task.

At first it irritated Bathsheba that her older sister was so competent at shirking her fair share of the women's work of the place. Rachel was always the first one in the buggy to go visiting, and the last one to don a coverall when someone was needed to supervise the recounting and restacking of a storeroom. But her aunt soothed Bathsheba with due praise. She also answered as many of Bathsheba's questions as Bathsheba could wish — as long as the questions related to household matters. And Bathsheba's father occasionally rewarded Bathsheba by calling her his busy little housekeeper. It gave her a confused twinge of embarrassment, but at least it was a compliment that he never paid to Rachel.

Thus Bathsheba enjoyed some privileges which came with her aunt's and her father's regard, and she took satisfaction from the household competence which she was gradually acquiring.

Her training was temporarily interrupted by two years at the Lanchard Seminary for Young Ladies in Savannah. Aunt Mary insisted upon it, even though it meant that she would be without her niece's assistance for much of that interim. On the eve of her seminary stay, her father counselled her to be a credit to her family and to write home every week. Bathsheba listened to him carefully: she especially felt her obligation to him for his largesse. He had sold a fine darkie pair — a sturdy brother and sister — in order to pay for it.

She took his counsel to heart, and greatly improved her command of French while at the seminary. She excelled at it there, jabbering with other similarly–inclined girls in a blissful orgy of irregular verbs. Admittedly, much of their skill was initially acquired while vying to impress the somewhat moody and much too handsome Monsieur Refay, who was their French Master until Miss Lanchard could no longer tolerate his increasingly obvious attentions to the music teacher. He was dismissed, but by then Bathsheba was fairly caught by the beauty of the French language, and she pursued her studies under the less inspiring tutelage of the dour and decidedly unhandsome Mademoiselle Johnson.

Bathsheba's weekly letters home from the seminary were laden with the fruits of her lingual accomplishments. If her mother had been alive, Bathsheba was sure that all of her letters would have been promptly answered. As it was, only Aunt Mary occasionally sent her a hurried note, which never referred to the many things that Bathsheba had written home about.

This lack of connection puzzled Bathsheba until she discovered its cause during her first visit home from the seminary. She found several of her letters in a drawer of the hall chiffonier, unopened.

"Oh, it got to where we couldn't understand what was in them," her sister Rachel had purred when Bathsheba asked her why nobody had opened them.

Bathsheba went about the house gathering up all of her neglected and disregarded missives. She found most of them under the newspapers and agricultural journals; one she retrieved from inside one of her younger brother's new boots, where he had placed it to fill out an ill–fitting heel. Then she spent the afternoon in the decrepit treehouse, way out near where the darkies were chopping cotton in the fields. With the steady fall of their hoes wafting past her hideaway, she smoothed the edges of her letters fondly and re–read some of them. She had spent such energies upon them, searching for the drollest quips in French and English to enliven the thin news from her cloistered seminary life. Each letter took days to compose, written and re–written until, in Bathsheba's eyes, the dull fare of existence had been transformed by her perseverance and occasional inspiration into scintillating — or at least engaging — or at least mildly interesting — ingots of entertainment for her family's enjoyment. It had taken artistry, perhaps even a touch of genius. The least they could have done was try to appreciate her efforts.

92

With such pride and satisfaction she had addressed each letter to her family, placing one every week without fail on the mail tray in the seminary's front hall. With such pleasure had she imagined their reception — she was sure her letters would be read aloud at the dinner table, and passed from hand to hand, with every family member there to chortle indulgently over each new proof of her budding wit. She imagined that even some of the house darkies would partake of the gaiety, straining to overhear the content of her letters between their trips to and from the kitchen. They would purse their lips to hold back smiles at her cleverness, and enjoy it in secret. Even Rachel could not fail to be impressed by and, perhaps, a little jealous of, her sister's obvious gift for language.

But her words didn't look very nimble on that singular afternoon, strewn in laboriously penned pages across her skirts, beloved only by their disappointed author. Perhaps there was a little too much French in them, she was willing to admit. She began to notice that every sentence in English was followed by at least one in French. That, in retrospect, was probably more French than one could reasonably expect one's family to mine for the nuggets of cleverness buried within. But still, they could have at least read the parts that were in their own language, even if somebody else's afternoon teas, and the peeves of wearisome instructresses, didn't particularly appeal to them. It was the observing eye, coupled with the exquisite — or at least capable — turn of phrase which mattered when one had such slight material to work with. They should, at least, have bothered to open them and read them, out of love and consideration for her.

But no, it wasn't to be. Her family could not be relied upon to appreciate the fruit of her labors, the harvest of her oeil d'observation and her French studies. She mulled over her unappreciative relations while the darkies worked the field, some of them barely fifteen feet from her dilapidated refuge. She stared over their bent backs, which occasionally shimmered through a welling of tears, for what seemed like a long time. But gradually the swing of their hoes, keeping time with a monotonous work song, soothed her wounded heart wonderfully. When the last of them were beyond her retreat she stole away, oddly refreshed by their slow progress through the hot, dusty fields.

When she returned to the seminary after that holiday she continued to write to her family as faithfully and as diligently as she had before discovering their utter indifference to her correspondence. Her spirits did sometimes flag as she labored over particularly difficult turns of phrase, but that never kept her from regularly depositing her weekly offering on the silver mail tray.

On her next visit home she found that Joseph had put all of her letters into the top drawer of the hall chiffonier for her, and from there she retrieved them, every one of them crisp and unopened. She immediately suspected that he had put them in the drawer as soon as they arrived. But no, he assured her, he had left each one out "til I pick up de nex un from town, Missy."

On that second visit home Bathsheba duly set aside an afternoon to read through her letters, but thereafter on visits home she only collected them from the drawer and put them away with the others. The latter ones were actually better, she knew, than her earlier efforts. She had, for instance, learned to use her beloved French with more moderation and discretion. But read them she could not. Her family's indifference was too palpable for her to overcome it.

Upon finding herself in the 1990s, Bathsheba sometimes wondered what had ever happened to those letters. Apart from a small oil sketch of her done at age ten by a traveling portrait painter, those letters were her sole tangible remains after her disappearance in 1859. Had anyone ever read them, she wondered, after she was thought to be drowned?

Would Rachel have found them and read some of them? Never, Bathsheba was certain. She'd stop at the first French word she came across.

Her brothers? No, they never read anything except the horse news in the papers.

Father? Aunt Mary? They were much too busy with the running of the plantation. No, it was very likely that nobody ever read them. After her 'death' they would have gone into the attic, moldering there until the 1890s when the house burned to the ground.

*   *   *

After her graduation from the seminary, Bathsheba returned home to resume her position as her aunt's stalwart helper in managing the household, with one important difference. Aunt Mary had determined that Bathsheba was ready to take more responsibility in managing the servants.

Her aunt was adamant on the need for a firm hand to avert their natural "sloth and waywardness". With the house servants the challenge was subtle: these were mostly older slaves, capable ones who valued the relative ease and security that came with working in the big house. They would exert themselves well enough — usually — to keep favor with the acolyte mistress who, they knew, might someday have a much fuller power over them. The order among them had long since been established, and Bathsheba had only to learn the ranking well enough to effectively control them. When the fireplaces were not properly swept up and laid for the next chill morning, Bathsheba learned to go directly to Mabel about it, rather than to chastise the little house maid who had neglected or forgotten her job. Mabel ruled the younger house and laundry servants with a sharper tongue than Bathsheba could ever hope to acquire.

But the yard and ferry slaves were another matter: they were a more unruly lot which required much more skill and, at times, force. They were not as strictly ordered as the house servants, in part because their work varied more, but also because they had not been well supervised in the past. They constantly shirked work — though not openly enough, usually, to risk a whipping. Their work always took longer, and the yields were always lower, when they were not strictly and closely supervised.

A year–round foreman had been tried off and on since Aunt Mary had come to stay. But after each trial Aunt Mary found that she much preferred her own management, despite the strain on her nerves, to that of a sandhiller or — worse — one of the more reliable slaves. At cotton harvest of course the most capable overseers from the fields took over the ginning and most of the ferrying. But during the rest of the year, when the ferry business was not hectic and the warehouses were never more than half full, Aunt Mary was in charge and Bathsheba, after her return from the seminary, was her up and coming assistant.

It took sharp eyes to catch the shortages before the yields had passed though enough hands to obviate blame for them. And it took a quick keen mind to track where each slave was supposed to be, and

95

to gage when each should have finished one task and be ready for the next. Aunt Mary's eyes and mind were keen enough, and she took some pride in her God–given abilities to rule the slaves.

The job also required a willingness to occasionally use the whip. Aunt Mary had one, and was not unwilling to use it. Its grip had been pared down to better fit her hand, and she took a grim pride in carrying it looped on her skirtwaist when going about her work outside of the house. She wasn't too dainty to ensure the discipline of the yard and ferry with her own whip arm. She had never yet had to fetch an overseer from the fields to do the whipping for her.

She was careful not to expose herself to the criticism of the neighbors by doing her whipping in the heat of a passion, or too openly. She usually gaged when a whipping was due and planned it out shrewdly, for maximum effect among the slaves, and to excite as little notice as possible among the people who were about the house or using the ferry.

Bathsheba in her aunt's wake proved to have reasonably sharp eyes for shortages, and a fairly keen mind for tracking the work of the yard. In the matter of the whip hand, though, Aunt Mary noted some reticence in her niece. At first she did not attempt to pressure her student: to some it came naturally; others needed to learn by sour experience to overcome squeamishness, in the higher cause of maintaining discipline and order.

But the slaves easily sensed Bathsheba's timidity and, like veteran illusionists they strove to distract her eyes from the yields, and to confuse her mind about their own whereabouts. Gradually they grew bolder. After a particularly sly triumph, some of them even dared to chortle, only partially hiding their glee in fake coughs, while the girl was still in earshot.

Aunt Mary had observed that the order and discipline were deteriorating when her niece was in charge, but she did not attempt to set things right for the girl. She bided her time, sensing that a turning point in her niece's education was bound to occur before long.

Then came the day when four large bags of grain were tipped into the river, seemingly by accident. A week earlier something similar had occurred, when a mule balked on the ferry and some old, damaged sugar barrels toppled into the river. The ferry had been at midstream at the time, and the barrels were soon too far downstream to be retrieved. The loss had been extremely embarrassing because the barrels belonged to a cracker tinker who was collecting them from the countryside to repair and resell in Savannah. Although he had paid almost nothing for them, he made Bathsheba's father pay dearly for his loss. He was loud and coarse, refusing to settle with Aunt Mary, insisting on either dealing with the 'man of the house', or going to law. He had completely disturbed the peace of the entire family by his uncouth hollering, and by the deposits of baccy juice that he and his older boy had left everywhere they had swaggered while waiting for their monetary damages, including on the Persia carpet in the main hall of the house.

This time a mule stumbled against some bags of grain that were stacked too high on the landing, and the four furthest out fell into the river. Bathsheba saw the mule rear, and there was something in the animal's sudden movement that made her suspect that the animal had been poked in some way by the slave leading it. It was subtle — just an odd lean by the man into the animal's under belly, when he was seemingly recovering from a stumble. And then the efforts by the darkies to retrieve the bags before they caught in the current — their jumping around and their shouts, was too much like an antic play, rather than a genuine effort to retrieve the bags.

Bathsheba stood beside the landing watching their movements and their faces, and listening to their noise. Aunt Mary was actually in their midst, ordering them sharply into pole some boats to pursue the bags, but that was the problem: she was too close to it to see the fakery of it. And their boat maneuvers only sent the bags further into the current.

Then Bathsheba turned quickly and found a negro near her who was grinning to himself. It was a knowing grin, a private one. He was partly behind a bale pile and probably had not expected anyone to see him.

Bathsheba scanned the river farther out and spied some cracker boys downriver. She rushed to the bluffs and ran scrambling along them, screaming and waving her arms like windmills at the boys.

"Grab those bags!" she screeched into a stiff breeze, waving and pointing excitedly. "Grab me one of them and I'll give you a silver dollar for it! A silver dollar!"

97

The boys stared at her, not making out her meaning at first. Then one of them finally caught on and they both paddled like mad and managed to pole their awkward craft into the way of one of the bags. What five negroes in two pole boats had failed to accomplish, the two eager cracker boys in their leaky tub achieved. They hooked one of the bags, half–submerged, alongside with a paddle, and flailed their floundering boat out of the current and over to the shore.

They were far down stream by the time they made shore, but Bathsheba had run along the bluffs and had scrambled down to their landing place to meet them. She knew that she was disheveled in a manner that a lady should allow herself to be, but just then it felt glorious, cut loose from all propriety by the sweat pouring out of her skin, and by her loosened hair whipping around her face in the hot breeze. She grinned at the boys when they reached shore as if she was one of them, and, nearly breathless, copiously thanked them. Then she asked them to drag the bag back to the landing for her.

When they arrived her aunt was waiting with most of the yard and ferry darkies assembled. She had kept them from scattering when Bathsheba had run off along the bluffs. The boys drug their sodden prize up to the stern woman, and Bathsheba herself took a bale hook and worried the stitching on the waterlogged bag until it tore open. Instead of containing grain, though, the bag held chaff with a scattering of small stones for added weight.

The farmer's grain had been bagged and weighed at the Severly mill the evening before. Bathsheba herself had seen it poured into the bags and weighed and marked. A cloudburst had delayed the transport of the grain until this morning. Overnight, though, the grain had disappeared from the bags, and this fill had been put into them.

Bathsheba stared at the contents of the bag and knew what had to be done. She took her time. She contemplated the knot of darkies and named three of them. Her aunt nodded and gave orders for them to be readied for their whipping, while Bathsheba took the cracker boys to the house for their silver dollar. Instead of one to be shared by both of them, though, she gave them one apiece, and she ordered the cook to feed them at the back door.

She didn't stop to fix her hair which was tumbling down her back, or to straighten her clothes. A taut silence ruled the house and the yard as she walked back down to the landing, and took her aunt's cord whip from her outstretched hand.

Momentum carried her through the first lash that she gave each prone figure. Then she faltered, never having been this close before to the splitting welts and the rivulets of glistening blood. Wordlessly her aunt took the whip back from her and snapped it to scatter the flies. Then she gave each man eleven lashes more with her surer, heavier whip arm. Salt water was poured over the wounds and the men were untied and dragged to the cabins. But the demonstration of power could not stop there. The work of the yard and ferry was grimly restarted and pursued.

The owner of the missing grain had a quieter disposition than the tinker who had lost his moldy barrels. He, his boy and his darkie had also witnessed the whipping. He readily settled with Bathsheba's aunt on the grain's worth and went on his way.

Bathsheba and her aunt did not say a word to each other about the whipping. But at dinner that evening Rachel had a great deal to say about it.

"We positively must put a stop to it," she railed. "It is much too unbecoming of a *lady* to be seen whipping the servants. Why, Bathsheba looked a perfect fright with her clothes all mused and her hair — I just quail to think of the tales that old farmer is going to make out about us. I say again that it's a man's job to run the yard and ferry, Aunt Mary."

"Name me the man who can do the job better than Bathsheba and I can, and I'll give him a trial," Aunt Mary said sedately over her chick peas, more to her brother–in–law than to his eldest daughter.

"And that's not all," Rachel swept on, ignoring Aunt Mary's rejoinder. "Buddy was in the stables showing Princess to the Meyer boys. "Well, naturally when they heard the commotion in the yard they all had to go over and gawk at it — you agree with me, don't you, Buddy?"

"Well, it was rather, um, embarrassing, Aunt Mary," Edward contributed, "to have one's friends see one's sister so, er, glowing — well, actually, so flushed in the face. Most girls of our kind just don't do that kind of thing. I think that you should have called in a field overseer to do it, Aunt Mary."

"Yes!" agreed Rachel. "That's exactly what *I* would have done."

99

"The overseers are much too busy with the fieldwork right now," Aunt Mary put in calmly. "And the ferry is not really their concern, at this time of the year. It's Bathsheba and I that the yard servants have to obey, Rachel, most of the time."

Aunt Mary then addressed her nephew.

"I had the stables checked beforehand, Edward. You must have come in afterward by the south door. Next time send someone down to see if there's anything going on in the yard. That's all you need do."

"Whipping doesn't have to be done very often," Aunt Mary then said to her brother–in–law. "And you all know well the cathartic effect that a good whipping has. I'll warrant that Bathsheba and I will not have any further trouble with the yard servants for quite some time."

The lord of the manor took his time before answering the combatants. On the one hand his industrious sister–in–law took a great deal of the work of running the place upon herself, and he was loathe to frustrate her unnecessarily. But on the other hand, Rachel had always been his favorite and he did not relish the genteel nagging which she was sure to persist in until she got her way in this.

"I will take the matter under consideration," he announced at length. "Perhaps it would be best to try out another foreman," he said with a nod toward Rachel, "if someone hardworking and trustworthy enough can be found," he continued with a nod in Aunt Mary's direction, "to lighten Mary and Bathsheba's work. And just what, Buddy, was the Meyer boys' opinion of our new mare?"

Over the next several days Aunt Mary kept Bathsheba very busy, and watched her closely for signs of nervous reaction to the whipping. She did not want Bathsheba to suffer any avoidable pangs of conscience from it, so she kept the girl's mind busy with their work and with enough diversions to reinforce Bathsheba's sense of having accomplished something essential. She saw to it that the yard and ferry ran particularly smoothly, and she assigned work to Bathsheba which took marked concentration. She also filled the girl's evenings with her store or reminisces from her own homeplace upriver, in Richmond County.

She even expressed an interest in relearning some French under her niece's tutelage. Bathsheba immediately undertook to prepare an

100

array of French verb exercises for her aunt's edification. But while this proved to be a welcome distraction for Bathsheba during the days after the whipping, her aunt never did manage to find the time to apply herself to them.

Bathsheba still couldn't help feeling some mental discomforts from the whipping she had administered. Sometimes in the moments before sleep her mind flashed up the long welts and the bright red curds that the whip brought up from the brown flesh. She curled into a miserable ball on her comfortable bed, and wished so hard that time could flow backward, to before Aunt Mary had come, to before her mother had died. If only mother had lived — Bathsheba was sure that her mother, who was against slavery, would not have let Bathsheba get involved with anything like a whipping.

But time would not flow backward. She could only go forward by thinking about how thieving was a sin that had to be punished. And she had punished it. In those particular circumstances, what else could she have done? Life as it was had to go on, as best it could.

Eventually the whipping incident faded from her day to day consciousness. The life of the plantation moved forward. And when, because of Bathsheba's efforts, Aunt Mary was not as weighed down by the responsibilities for the household and yard, she turned her energies toward a sorely neglected matter. She began to do more visiting, and over the course of several months she canvassed the county for a bachelor who might match the taste and social standing of her favorite niece Bathsheba.

Bathsheba's sister Rachel never lacked admirers, but Bathsheba usually did. Men's eyes tended to slip right past her at the holiday balls and the other local cotillions, and settle instead on Rachel. Bathsheba's features could be pleasing enough under favorable circumstances, but she was too retiring, and somehow lacked the verve that was essential to attract the young men of her class.

Bathsheba's aunt understood this: she herself was living out the consequences of this deficit, as a spinster aunt in her brother–in–law's home. But that which had not been overcome in her own instance, she was determined to compensate for in her niece Bathsheba's case.

The list of willing enough bachelors was quickly narrowed down to one solid candidate. Approaching 35 years of age, Douglas

Pritchard had been overlooked by most of the county's damsels due to an unfortunate reputation for having hopelessly ponderous parlor manners. He was too steady, too staid, too slow–moving and unimaginative to suit anyone of a romantic or selective disposition. But he was nonetheless the shrewd pick of Bathsheba's aunt, even before he unexpectedly won a local political contest. He was elected superior court judge when the incumbent unexpectedly angered the local political lords just days before the election.

The marriageable young ladies and their mothers and aunts immediately thought more kindly of Douglas's drawing room manners, and several of the mothers and aunts were quick to call upon his ailing mother. But they soon found that they were already too late: Bathsheba's aunt had been visiting the invalid for months before the election, and a friendship had sprung up between the staid spinster and the often querulous shut in. Mrs. Pritchard would have no part in disturbing the prior claim on her son's affection by dear Mary's niece. A few of the more determined damsels did not give up without first attempting to dislodge Bathsheba from Douglas's heart, but Douglas's unexpected surge of popularity did not turn his head. He proved strangely impervious to their insinuations and charms. With a humble but plodding constancy he soon made it abundantly clear that he would not forsake Bathsheba in favor of any admittedly more accomplished — and perhaps less eccentric — belle. He was inclined to be loyal, and Bathsheba's quirky ways had somehow engaged his heart. He fancied himself to be in love, and therefore the attempts to dislodge Bathsheba from his affections only served to strengthen his loyalty to her. Douglas promptly conversed with Bathsheba's father on the subject of his marrying Bathsheba, and soon thereafter Bathsheba, with her family's approval and encouragement, accepted his marriage proposal.

After the engagement was announced, Bathsheba's aunt often smiled quietly to herself when she happened to be chatting with one of the defeated contenders after church. Only she and Bathsheba knew that it had not merely been a matter of having gotten to Douglas Pritchard first.

There had been a number of complications, the first of which was that Douglas Pritchard's mother was a woman who had been dying of a heart ailment for over thirty years. Even after numerous solicitous visits, Bathsheba's aunt had not been able to coax Mrs. Pritchard into paying even one return call at Severly with her son, due to her wretchedly poor health. From her long acquaintance with illness and a disinclination to leave the comfort of her own home, Mrs. Pritchard had amassed countless facile ways to excuse herself from anything for which she did not have sufficient enthusiasm. It was not until Bathsheba's aunt accidentally discovered Mrs. Pritchard's keen interest in pea fowl that the coveted return visit was arranged: by a fortuitous coincidence, Severly had one of the finest of the few musters of pea fowl to be found anywhere in the Georgia uplands. In fact they were not a popular lawn ornament, due to their large and copious droppings, and the unearthly screeching of the males at night during their mating season.

The next complication became apparent soon after Mrs. Pritchard and Douglas were at long last seated in the best parlor at Severly: neither Douglas nor Bathsheba would speak. Douglas sat in silence next to his mother, inattentively gazing out the window. He displayed no discomfiture; apparently his mind was just elsewhere. There seemed to be no one in the room for whom he would bestir himself to speak.

Bathsheba sat in silence also, at first because she was too nervous to be able to think of anything to say, but eventually because of Douglas's patent indifference to her presence, which spurred her on toward a similar disinclination to converse.

Bathsheba's aunt persevered with the polite forms despite this overwhelming obstacle to her matchmaking plans. Several times Douglas almost spoke, drawn from his oblivious contemplation of the trees visible from the window, by her utmost conversational skill. But each time that his attention had been brought sufficiently around and he was about to speak, his mother, made impatient by his delay, spoke for him.

Finally while Mrs. Pritchard was distracted by a choice of tea biscuit, Aunt Mary managed to draw from Douglas his opinion of the weather. She then waited anxiously, and Bathsheba waited with a modicum of grudging interest, to hear what he had to say about it.

He spoke, but then another complication arose, for Douglas showed a disinclination to relinquish his hold upon the conversation once he had gained it. His erudition on the weather became

103

exhausting to audit. Eventually the frazzled Aunt Mary, who was usually the model of decorum, overthrew her principles and crudely interrupted him when he paused for breath, in order to give Bathsheba a chance to contribute to the subject. But Bathsheba, lulled by the drone of Douglas's voice, had been devising a French version of his weather commentary in her head. When startled from this laborious exercise by her aunt's desperate prompt, Bathsheba complied readily enough, but in French. Aunt Mary closed her eyes and gave an almost imperceptive shake of her head, while Douglas and his mother simply stared at Bathsheba.

They would have thought her erudition clever enough if they could have understood it, but they only looked blank when she at length finished. Neither of them, it was plain, knew a lick of French. In the inevitable conversational lull, which even Aunt Mary felt too discouraged to attempt to fill, Mrs. Pritchard finally renewed her earlier hints that she was ready to tour the pea fowl runs.

Aunt Mary led the way, thoroughly defeated, to the fowl yards. A pious resignation had settled into her breast. She had tried — the good Lord knew she had tried — to further her niece's matrimonial possibilities. But if despite her best efforts Bathsheba and Douglas could not improve upon the opportunity which she had gone to such trouble to provide to them, then it was beyond her skill and inclination to persist further. With an air of patient suffering she turned her full attention to providing Mrs. Pritchard with all of the arcane information about peacocks and peahens that the wheezing woman could possibly desire. Douglas maintained an impenetrable silence by his mother's side throughout the long tour, and Bathsheba when she spoke at all deliberately and perversely used rather too much French.

In this manner the visit ground down inescapably toward a flat, inglorious end. Mrs. Pritchard's withered cheeks were the only ones flushed with pleasure beside the Pritchard buggy, during the parting pleasantries between herself and Aunt Mary. Douglas stood by silently impervious, and Bathsheba fought hard to subdue several midafternoon yawns. For form's sake, Aunt Mary arranged an encouraging smile upon her face and turned to Douglas.

"Douglas," she said sweetly, though hopelessly, "your mother is too frail to visit us often, I know. But we do hope that you will come yourself, from time to time."

Douglas looked to his mother for a moment and, at an emphatic nod from her, ponderously replied.

"This Sunday then, if you please, after church."

Aunt Mary's knees almost buckled from the shock. Bless the boy — perhaps he was not as much of a dullard as he seemed. She dazedly answered that they would be expecting him. But as soon as the Pritchards were safely beyond the bend at the bottom of the lawn, Bathsheba informed her aunt that she planned to be ill on Sunday and therefore would not be able to see Mr. Pritchard when he called.

Aunt Mary wisely did not attempt to dissuade her niece. There would be five long days before the visit, five days for Bathsheba to weigh this particular man's boorish tendencies against the prospect of having no gentleman caller at all. And sure enough, by Sunday Bathsheba had decided to be at least well enough to greet her caller at the outset of his visit. She astutely reasoned that she could always have an attack of indisposition as soon as he became too boring to be endured.

Douglas duly came and Aunt Mary prudently kept the best parlor clear of everyone except herself, Douglas and Bathsheba. Then after some preliminary pleasantries she settled into a determined silence over some handwork, leaving Douglas and Bathsheba to find their own way through the shoals of early courtship.

During the past five days Aunt Mary had determined that she was too busy a woman to put much more effort into this unlikely match, and she was enough of a gambler to make a bold bid on a weak hand. She had thought it over, and decided to stake everything on her surmise that Douglas's hand was weaker than her own.

It was weaker. Much weaker. Douglas Pritchard had obtained fewer invitations to call upon young ladies as the years passed, and most of them had been socials where he had become too accustomed to sitting silent and inattentive in the background. Lately he had developed a vague dissatisfaction with this state of his affairs, but his experience gave him no insights for improving his position. His mother's only guidance in this latest instance was that he ought to call on Bathsheba a few times, to please Bathsheba's aunt. Bathsheba was a pleasant enough girl, his mother said, though it would be an improvement if she could restrict herself to her native tongue.

Thus Douglas Pritchard came to be sitting in the best parlor at Severly on that Sunday afternoon with a sense of readiness for something, but at a complete loss on how to partake in its accomplishment.

Silence inevitably reigned. It was broken only by bursts of merriment which occasionally floated through the halls from the other parlor, where the rest of the Severly family and Rachel's current beau were ensconced. Douglas stared out the window, Bathsheba conjugated irregular French verbs in her head, and Aunt Mary made remarkable progress on a braidwork dress front for one of her younger nieces, which had been languishing in her work basket so long that the girl was probably getting a little too old for it..

But Bathsheba eventually tired of conjugating French verbs on the uncomfortable sofa and decided that the time had come to end her part in this largely speechless enterprise.

"I am feeling a bit indisposed," she announced while crossing her shawl over her chest and hunching over, "in my stomach. I think I shall have to retire for the rest of the afternoon. Vraiment, il est temps de quitter ce paty."

Aunt Mary kept her eyes steadily on her stitching and her lips firmly closed.

"Oh?" replied Douglas after a long interval. "I wonder if your indisposition stems from a germ that has invaded your, er, your body."

"A . . . what?" Bathsheba asked.

"A germ. I wonder if you have heard of it, the new scientific theories of germs? From Europe?"

Without giving Bathsheba a chance to reply, Douglas then launched into a detailed account of the newly disseminated theories about germs and bacteria which were being advanced by some progressive doctors, in lieu of the humoral view of bodily ailments. Douglas had been told of these developments by Doctor Samuels, who came regularly from Augusta to attend upon his mother. Dr. Samuels was a young man who had been trained in Philadelphia, and Douglas had been intrigued as well by his theories of misshapen blood cells and irregular tissues. Over the course of time he had accumulated an impressive understanding of the new theories, and he saw no reason not to present this trove of knowledge in the Severly parlor.

It was given a remarkably better reception than his weather discourse had received several days before. Bathsheba had a fascination for arcane knowledge. The only interruptions that he encountered when he sometimes paused over long for a breath were some remarkably intelligent questions from Bathsheba, which encouraged him to lengthen rather than shorten his presentation.

He felt an unaccustomed contentment when he at last found nothing more to say on the subject, and his final pause generated no additional questions from a similarly satisfied Bathsheba. The ensuing silence was an oddly serene one. Aunt Mary snipped a thread tail and smiled quietly over the completed bodice. Her intuitive culling of the bachelor list was proving out after all. Her cultivation of Mrs. Pritchard had produced at last a promising young seedling. Though it was still up to Douglas and Bathsheba to care for the tender plant and to bring it to an adequate fruition.

Aunt Mary had few illusions. Douglas and Bathsheba would make a rather odd couple at best. But not necessarily, she thought, an ill–suited one, nor a particularly unhappy one.

There were of course many details to be worked out between Douglas and Bathsheba. Both had considerable adjustments to make. Douglas's tendency to veer between complete silence and the opposite extreme of encyclopedic erudition — that clearly required some regulation. To this end Bathsheba used the expedient of a stomach indisposition to great effect. Whenever she announced a recurrence of that ailment Douglas was by degrees brought to understand that he had been either too long silent or far too discursive for her taste. And he was concerned enough for her health and her good opinion of him to anticipate the onset of the affliction and forestall it. He came to watch her shawl during their time together, instead of the scenery beyond the windows. Then Bathsheba had only to gather her shawl ends preparatory to crossing them, and Douglas would switch from silence to speaking, or from speaking to an abrupt silence, as the particular instance would dictate. For he had a soundly analytical mind to apply to a problem once his

107

interest in it was sufficiently engaged. The result of his attention to Bathsheba's shawl was that between them they achieved after several months a passable approximation of a normal conversation.

Bathsheba for her part had to be judicious in her use of her shawl. She greatly preferred his discourses on the sciences: the new germ and cell theories, the discovery and naming of the planet Neptune, and even scientific applications, like the self–governing windmill, and the new chemical cooling. For these her shawl would usually lay limp and forgotten at her elbows. But Douglas's interests were much broader, and the notion of fair play which they shared required Bathsheba to listen to more of Douglas's lengthy opinions on the politics of the day and about the local crops than she would have otherwise felt able to endure.

Bathsheba also had to make another sacrifice, for Douglas took a dislike to her use of the French language in their conversations. Her love of the language was such that she persisted in using it until Douglas adopted the expedient of answering her French with his Greek. Only then did Bathsheba realize that she was going to have to choose between this particular beau and her beloved French. She considered, and she chose. French lost.

The courtship progressed quietly, steadily until several months before the primaries for the 1858 elections. Then it was interrupted somewhat by Douglas's efforts to make himself known as a candidate.

Douglas had been chosen to run against the popular incumbent, who had been the circuit's superior court judge for sixteen years. Most of the local gentry were well satisfied with the incumbent; they considered him to be just coming into his prime as the arbitrator of their land, slave and domestic disputes. Thus no one expected Douglas to win, least of all Douglas himself. He had only agreed to be on the ballot because Colonel Moss, one of his few large clients, asked him to. Colonel Moss was an older man of unbending principles, and one of his precepts happened to be that no candidate for local office should ever run unopposed. No matter that he himself was backing the incumbent: the form, if not the fact, of democracy was to be duly maintained. Many in the county agreed with him. Anything less would be too much like a horse race with but one horse running.

Douglas too had principles. Despite the near certainty of his defeat, he nonetheless felt it his duty to make himself known as a candidate. Thus for several months before the election he split his spare hours between Bathsheba's sweetening company and the work of all hours, introducing himself to as many of the county's farmers and merchants, the great and the small — at least, as many of them as were willing to give him a hearing. The planters and the factors and the towns' upper crust were, on the whole, patiently indulgent with him; many of them rather appreciated his neophyte efforts to uphold the forms. The smaller farmers and the crossroad store keeps tended to be more dismissive: they were more likely to think that Douglas was a fool. How else could they reconcile the time that he devoted to the useless pursuit of their votes?

But Douglas persevered, all the while accepting the near certainty of defeat with becoming stoicism and modesty.

And then came the sudden reverse in his opponent's popularity, in the eleventh hour before the election. In a testamentary dispute between two half–brothers he had handed down a decision in favor of the brother who had outraged the community by moving his mulatto concubine into his home as soon as his father died, despite the strenuous objections of his wife and adult white children. It did not matter that the probate law and the relevant facts clearly supported the judge's decision. It did not matter that the dispute was over a specific bequest for a small piece of infertile land, which had previously been owned by the victor's mother.

It did matter that the mulatto slave woman was probably the man's half–sister, and that due to the wife's vociferousness the judge had to have known this. And it did matter that the victor's wife and his defeated half–brother were both many times better connected to the county's elite than he was, or could ever hope to be.

The judge had felt that the property involved was too insignificant to generate a political upheaval. So he had simply decided the case on its merits. But within days of the decision the judge found himself vilified as being of the same ilk as the victorious litigant. His sanity and morals were questioned. And many people wondered aloud whether he had become an abolitionist.

In vain he asserted the principle of law that he had applied to the case. In vain he informed everyone who would listen that he himself abhorred the winner's morals. His years of dedicated public service were entirely forgotten in the simmer of public outrage, which was kept agitated by the winner's spurned wife. Clearly, social rather than legal justice was demanded. In the public record the victor could not be made to pay the price, but the judge could. He was not going to be allowed to make any more such mistakes.

The planters and factors turned against their candidate, and considered their options. Douglas was hastily summoned and sniffed over, and sounded out on his principles. When asked about how he would have disposed of the half–brothers' case, Douglass answered with confident simplicity that though he had not had an opportunity to study the facts and the law in depth, that surely there must be some precedent somewhere to support a more acceptable outcome for a case like theirs. The county's elite was satisfied, and the word went out that Douglas would do. He was deemed fit enough for the office under the circumstances, and was duly elected.

Thus his star rose and, though awed at first by the unexpected social prominence that came with the being judge elect, he rapidly became accustomed to his more exalted position among the important men of the community. But what strengthened Bathsheba's heart toward him was that he retained his former modest opinion of himself with respect to womankind. He remained the same Douglas as before in his deference to his mother and in his deepening regard for Bathsheba. No effort to dislodge her from his heart could succeed. Even Rachel's increasingly serious attempts to snatch her sister's beau were met with a studied imperviousness, until Aunt Mary noticed what Rachel was doing and put a firm end to them altogether.

* * *

During her first weeks in the 1990s Bathsheba sometimes missed Douglas exceedingly, when she remembered how very fond of each other they had become in the months before she had . . . supposedly drowned.

But much of the time she utterly despised him. How *could* he have married her insufferable sister?! How *could* he have ever reconciled himself to Rachel's flirty, shallow ways, after having imbibed in Bathsheba's obviously superior intellect and character?

110

Admittedly Rachel had parlor charms, but she had never even pretended to take the more important things of life seriously. Like book learning, and household duties. The ordering of the stars in the heavens, and the germs that infused all living things. Douglas *must* have been able to discern these differences between the sisters — one dross, the other gold. But against all reason, against all justice to Bathsheba, he had settled upon Rachel after Bathsheba was gone.

Male stupidity was the answer. Male weakness was the answer. Rachel's conniving was the answer. Bathsheba hated them both. How she *wished* she could go back to 1859 and stop everything, stop Douglas's confused, aimless sorrowing over her supposed demise. "I'm back!" she would shout, joyously running toward Douglas across the green expanse of Severly lawn, through scattering pea fowl. "I didn't drown!" she'd cry when she reached him, and she'd yank Rachel from his arm and slap her hussy sister's slack face. "How dare you!" she'd scream. She imagined flinging Rachel to the ground, and Rachel fighting back. They would roll, clawing and pulling and kicking around Douglas's feet. "How dare you!" she'd pant through her teeth. "I hate you!" she'd spit.

"Theba! Theba! Stop punching me! Crips! Help me! Somebody help me!"

Amongst the voices and confusion closing in on her, Bathsheba realized that something did not match up. The male voice behind the strong arms pulling her off Rachel — that was not Douglas's voice, or her father's or any of her brothers'. And the female voices swirling around her — they were not her aunt's or her sister's. The hands restraining her were black hands, the eyes bearing down on her were dark orbs in black faces. The slaves had revolted! Lord have mercy the slaves were attacking her in her bed!

"Help!" Bathsheba screamed hysterically, struggling to get free. "Murder! Help!"

"Theba! Calm yourself," Mrs. Bale said evenly. "No one's going to murder you."

And then it dissolved of course. Bathsheba blinked at the faces around her with delayed comprehension. Mauri and Stan and their mother. She shuddered with relief and the strenuous tautness left her. Stan released her arms.

"I'm sorry," Bathsheba murmured. "I was . . . dreaming."

111

"Do you have to be so physical in your dreams?!" Mauri demanded. "It was like you were trying to kill me or something!"

"It was my sister again," Bathsheba mumbled.

"Geez," Mauri muttered. "Makes me glad *I* never had one."

Bathsheba nodded shakily, hugging herself. "Most sisters wouldn't marry your beau though," she whispered.

"Well, that's all over with," Mrs. Bale stated flatly, calmly. "Let's all go back to bed. Remember, family meeting at ten o'clock this morning. Sharp."

Family meetings, Mauri had explained to Bathsheba, were held now and then to discuss matters of pressing concern. And the subject of this one was Bathsheba's future. She had recovered from her cold and had been with them for two weeks. Now it was time to consider her options and to make plans.

The meeting began promptly at 10.

"Leo will sell us a birth certificate for Theba," Stan reported. "Says it belonged to someone from upstate who died overseas."

"Can we trust this guy?" Mauri asked. "I mean, what's to stop him from selling the same birth certificate to several other people too?"

"I had the same question," Stan admitted. "But Leo isn't the kind of dude who provides credentials. It's a take–it or leave–it proposition. As it is I had to give him sixty dollars just to hold it for me until Tuesday. I have to pay him — used twenties and tens — on Tuesday or, he says, it's up for grabs. Somebody else might get it."

"May I inquire," Bathsheba asked, "what the name on this birth certificate is?"

Stan winced. "You're not going to like it," he told her. "And I might as well tell you right now that you won't like being only 16 years old again either."

"But I'm, I'm almost twenty–four."

"Leo was fresh out of birth certificates for twenty–four year olds."

Bathsheba stared at him dolefully.

"Look," Stan continued, "this is the best I could do. None of the guys who sell these things live in the better neighborhoods, or even in the so–so ones. You start out thinking that with your brains and with the money that you're going to spend, you ought to have some kind of leverage. But by the time you've sat in the guy's scuzzy apartment for two hours waiting for him, waiting while his woman nods off and a couple of kids trash the place playing kill the cops — by the time he gets back and has screamed at the woman and the kids and you're talking to him and noticing the bulge under his jacket that's a gun — by that time you'll take anything he's got just to get out of there in one piece."

"So I'm going to be sixteen again," Bathsheba said after a pause. "And my name is going to be . . .?"

"Sunrise Shansky."

"Ah, Sunrise?" Bathsheba asked. "That's a . . . that's a name?"

"Her parents must have been hippies or something."

"Hippies?" Bathsheba asked.

"I'll explain that later. For now, what we've got to decide is whether to take this birth certificate or not. Do I go back to this place on Tuesday with the money strapped to my sweating body, or do we try something else?"

After some discussion they opted to take a chance on the name. "And if this guy doesn't cheat us then you can always change the name itself later," Stan said, trying to comfort Bathsheba. "You can go to court and get it formally changed to something you like better. After you get your social security number and everything, then you can change all that to match the new name. Nobody'd ever blame you."

"Alright," Mrs. Bale said, "that's settled. Next is schooling. Bathsheba is willing to take the G.E.D., and we've estimated that it will take her about three, maybe four months of concentrated study to prepare for it." She pulled a thick softcover prep book from the sideboard shelf.

Bathsheba and I have already looked through this. She's going to need intense preparation in almost every subject area, but especially in math and history."

Mauri, Stan and their mother divvied up all the subjects she'd need help with. They also projected that if she passed the G.E.D. the first time, then she could take some summer courses at City College, unmatriculated. "And if she does well in those courses then they can be applied toward a degree later on," Mauri commented.

"So she has several options once she passes the G.E.D.," Mrs. Bale stated. "Now comes the matter of employment."

"Probably not worth the trouble until she has a social security number," Stan commented. "How long will it take to get that?"

"That was on my list to check," contributed Mauri. "Probably about a month, if there are no problems with that birth certificate."

"She could just study for the G.E.D. in the meantime," Stan shrugged. "We'll give her plenty of reading and study exercises to do."

"I think not," said Mrs. Bale crisply, and all eyes turned her way.

"Theba, you're very fact–oriented," Mrs. Bale continued. "So I expect you'll do well on the tests. If you don't pass the first time, then you will the next. It's the other part of you that I'm thinking about. The part that has to learn how to get along in this world, so that you can make your own way."

"A lot will rub off on her once she's in college . . .," Mauri suggested, but Mrs. Bale shook her head.

"You're thinking like somebody who has grown up in the last quarter of this century, Mauri. No, Bathsheba needs a real world base before she does any college work. If there's too much of a gap she won't be able to bridge it. She must get out and mix with people more, right from the beginning. We shouldn't keep her in a cocoon here with us."

"Ah, apparently you already have a plan," Stan stated.

"Yes," his mother agreed with a small smile. "I've looked into a few possibilities for volunteer work. Theba, which one of these do you think you'd . . ."

Bathsheba listened carefully and tried to choose wisely. Something that wasn't too difficult to master. Something that wouldn't interfere with her G.E.D. studies. Something where she could meet lots of different people, without being asked too many personal questions.

Chapter 10

"Sunrise? Sunrise Shansky?"

"Er, yes. Yes, ma'am."

"Come right this way. Funny name Sunrise. Your parents hippies or somethin'?"

"Ah, yes, ma'am."

"The name's Deb. Grab an apron. We'll be doing potatoes first."

Deb led Bathsheba to the back of the long room, past battered sinks and worktables, stoves and several massive refrigerators and freezers. Every surface was worn, scratched or stained, but everything smelled and looked very clean.

At the back of the room Deb handed Bathsheba a paring knife, and motioned her to a stool in front of large tubs of Eastern Golds.

"These'll be for boilin'. They've already been scrubbed, so all's we have to do is pick out the bad spots an' drop 'em into that big pot." Deb drew up another stool and together they whittled at the potatoes with their knives. Deb carved with an easy assurance, finishing two or three potatoes for every one of Bathsheba's.

"So your people was hippies?" Deb asked.

"Well," Bathsheba began cautiously, trying to blend fact and fiction into a usable whole, "my mother died when I was little, and I've, well, kind of lost . . . um, contact with my father."

"Oh?"

"Yes. I haven't seen him for . . . oh, quite a few years. That is, in a manner of speaking."

Deb looked at Bathsheba sharply. 'In a manner of speaking' . . . strange. What kind of distinction was this frumpy–looking white girl trying to make? "Speakin' of speakin'," Deb said out loud, "you talk like you're from down South."

"Yes. I'm from Georgia. Have you ever, ah, visited Georgia?" Bathsheba asked nervously.

"Mmm, depends on what you mean by visit. Passed through it a couple of times on my way to Disney World with the kids. Never left the interstate though. We were in too much of a hurry to get to where we were goin'."

Bathsheba relaxed a little and breathed somewhat more evenly. She also made a mental note to ask Mauri what Disney World was.

"But my brother did most of his Army time at Fort Hunter, near Savannah," Deb continued. "Married a Georgia gal, an' she talks somethin' like you do."

"Oh," Bathsheba said faintly. "Imagine that."

"Yep. Gladys is always tellin' us Georgia stuff, and we always laughing about it 'cause she make it all sound real cute. Like all them wild and wooly ghost stories. Like the one about the door painted blue that wasn't blue the next mornin', and the floatin' ghost–woman without a stitch on, with her can of paint, that nobody — now ain't that just perishin'?" said Deb with guffaw.

"Mmm . . ." replied Bathsheba, trying and failing to match Deb's merriment. She also had no idea what was so funny whether a door was painted blue or not. "Oh, perishing. Very perishing indeed."

An uneasy silence ensued. Deb and Bathsheba frowned at their potatoes. Deb was thinking about how stiff this white girl was, especially for someone whose parents were hippies. Bathsheba was realizing that if she waited, Deb was just going to ask more questions, that she might have trouble answering.

"Ah, have you always lived around here?" she asked Deb. "Around New York City?"

"Brooklyn born and bred," Deb answered. "Bedford Stuy. Ever been there?"

"No."

"Where you livin' then?"

"I've only been in the area for a few weeks actually. I'm staying with my, um, cousins in, in Queens, I think it is." Bathsheba's hands fluttered a bit over her potato. Somehow the conversation had gotten right back to herself. She tried again.

"Have you been helping out in this kitchen for long?" she asked Deb.

"At least ten year now, but only for Thanksgivin' and Christmas. Thanksgivin' always big here, see, and then I do the Christmas dinner so that more of the regulars can be home with their families then."

"You mentioned that you had kids," Bathsheba prompted, "when you were talking about passing through Georgia." That, at last, kept Deb's tongue busy for a while. Bathsheba relaxed a little while Deb spoke of loopy teachers, a hair craze and some kind of athletics called blading.

After the potatoes Bathsheba was moved on to other chores, like chopping celery for the turkey stuffing. More volunteers arrived and the kitchen began to hum with chatter and activity. The morning wore on into afternoon. Deb had left Bathsheba with some other volunteers and taken on more of the organizing with another older volunteer named Sue. Deb's and Sue's voices got louder and more assertive as the afternoon passed into evening.

"Not that pot, honey. That bigger one. Scour it out best you can. It'll have t'do. Hit's the only one big enough, see?"

"You gotta turn up them yams from the bottom to get the brown sugar mashed in good. Here, lemme show you."

Deb and Sue were the herders. They took their directions from the two kitchen supervisors, but they already knew much of what needed to be done. They prodded the other volunteers with their vocal patter into the timing needed for bringing together the masses of raw ingredients for the soup kitchen's Thanksgiving dinner.

Deb and Sue's directions were followed readily, willingly for the most part, even when their voices rose to a din and chopped sharp.

"We gotta get more o' them carrots and onions in around those birds."

"If you wanna get outta here tonight you gotta hustle, girl," Deb barked at Bathsheba. Bathsheba was tired but she set her jaw and pushed herself on. It was only her imagination, she told herself again and again, that Deb was singling her out for criticism.

Deb's voice had gotten rough and sour. Her face was sweaty and grim. They were falling well behind where they had to be in order to get everything done. They had to work faster, better. Bathsheba was forcefully reminded of the Severly overseer when Deb cracked a long spoon down on a pot rim next to Bathsheba's face. The sharp clatter produced a sudden lull in the kitchen buzz.

117

"Who the hell's been puttin' too much salt in this?" Deb demanded, outraged, eyeing the cardboard barrel of white crystals next to Bathsheba.

"That's salt?" Bathsheba asked weakly. "Why, I thought it was . . . that is . . ."

"Sunrise, I thought I tole you jus' to stir this. Did I say anything about adding something to it?"

"Well, I just thought . . . and that lady over there was putting some of this in hers . . . and . . ."

One of the kitchen supervisors — the smaller one — was already on her way over to rescue Bathsheba from the spluttering Deb.

"Not to worry," she told Deb while firmly guiding Bathsheba away from the ruined cranberry sauce. "We use it next week, in a special salsa sauce." She steered Bathsheba over to the napkins and silverware.

"I'm sorry," Bathsheba began. "I'm really very —"

"Deb mean well," Mrs. Rodriguez whispered to Bathsheba. Bathsheba had to crouch a little and lean over to hear what she was saying. "It's just that we have less help this year than usual, and there's still much to be done. Is a lot of people to feed tomorrow, yes?"

"Oh. I — really, I — I don't take any offense," Bathsheba said, even though she *did* take offense. She *did* resent Deb's bossing — Deb, a tyrant, a great big negress bossing her around — her, someone from an important family. A family that —"

"Is no problem. All fixed," Mrs. Rodriguez was saying. She was watching Bathsheba shrewdly, her dark eyes darting from the girl's set jaw to her mulish eyes. "All Deb want is for everybody to have a good meal here tomorrow," Mrs. Rodriguez continued carefully. "You wait. You see. Deb, she gonna give everybody big, big hug tomorrow when everything all ready. Even you. Especially you."

A thin whine unconsciously escaped from Bathsheba as she glanced at Deb, who was still muttering over the ruined pot of sauce. When she looked back at Mrs. Rodriguez she rolled her eyes and Mrs. Rodriguez laughed at her kindly. "You will see," she said and left Bathsheba with the forks, knives and spoons for rolling into bundles with paper napkins.

But soon afterward a voice behind Bathsheba made her jump. "Sunrise!" Deb barked. "Get your skinny butt over here and help with the potato n' spinach casseroles, will ya? Silverware can be rolled in the morning."

"Oh?" Bathsheba asked, standing up to face Deb. "You want my help? You think maybe I can help now without ruining everything?"

"Sunrise —," Deb bellowed with harried exasperation, her eyes flashing angrily. The kitchen clatter lulled. Everybody was listening.

"This is my first day here and I don't appreciate being yelled at by anybody," Bathsheba quavered, "even if I made a, well, a mistake."

Then Deb laughed. She laughed, shaking her head and then she sat down at the table.

"Sit down," she ordered Bathsheba, and after some belligerent hesitation Bathsheba sat down next to her. The kitchen clatter reasserted itself and they were private again.

Deb picked up some silverware and started rolling it up. "The first time I helped out here," she told Bathsheba, "I was movin' too fast, and a big bowl of onions just flew out of my hands, and those onions bounced all over everywhere. And old Ms. Slater, she 'bout ripped my head off about it. An' I was real mad at her, so mad that I almost walked out right then. But one of the supervisors calmed me down, and I was glad I stayed, because it was worth it the next day, seeing all of them people eatin' everything up."

"You understand?" Deb asked Bathsheba, turning to face her at the same time. "You understand?"

Bathsheba understood. She understood that Deb was kind of sorry about yelling at her, but that she wasn't going to apologize or change her attitude no matter what. Bathsheba was still angry, but Deb had said the right thing. She had reminded Bathsheba of the people that were coming to eat there tomorrow.

"Well," Bathsheba told Deb, "okay."

They finished about eight p.m., everyone hustling to leave, so as to be there bright and early the next day for the final preparations. Bathsheba had called for a ride home about a half hour earlier and stood waiting just outside the door.

"Remember," Deb exhorted everyone as they were leaving. "Everybody dress neat but comfortable. Long hair tied back, and no frip frap in your hair. Those kind of things always gonna fall in the gravy." Some of the volunteers laughed.

"You as good as your name?" Deb asked Bathsheba as she passed her.

"I beg your pardon?"

"You an early riser?" Deb asked. "Now, don't try to tell me that you don't get that question a lot."

"Oh! You mean my — you mean Sunrise," Bathsheba answered. "Well, no — I mean yes — that is, I don't get up particularly early. Actually, I've been thinking about changing my name to something more . . . comfortable. I've never really liked Sunrise."

Deb fidgeted, obviously anxious to leave. And Bathsheba wished she would go. But, "What would you change your name to?" Deb asked restlessly.

"Well, um, I've been thinking about, ah, maybe Bathsheba."

"Bath — what?" Deb asked.

"It's a name from the Bible. Old Testament."

"Oh? I wouldn't know much about that. I'm a Black Muslim myself."

"A Black Muslim," repeated Bathsheba, not knowing what else to say.

"Yeah. An' I been thinkin' about changing my name too. Maybe something like Sharifa."

Bathsheba tried to imagine Deb with the name Sharifa, and failed.

"You don't like it," Deb stated.

"Well, it's just . . . I'd have to get used to it," Bathsheba admitted.

"Bath — whatever–it–was — that's pretty weird too." Deb grinned, but Bathsheba couldn't tell whether she was teasing or serious.

Stan came up then and saved her from having to make any more small talk. Bathsheba introduced Stan to Deb. "We're, ah, cousins," Bathsheba added simply.

Deb looked deliberately from Bathsheba to Stan and then back. "There's somethin' weird about you girl," Deb then said. "I can just feel it."

"Indeed," Bathsheba said faintly.

"Yes." Deb shook her head though. "See you tomorrow then," she said stiffly, and she walked off down the street.

"Stan, do Black Muslims disapprove of miscegenation?" Bathsheba asked as they went to the car.

"I'm not sure. Could be. It's a fairly conservative religion. Why?"

"Just, um, curious. And I'm also wondering if you know anything about a Disney World."

Stan smiled. "That's a little easier."

The next morning Mauri, Stan and Mrs. Bale went with Bathsheba to the mission to help serve the Thanksgiving Day dinner. Bathsheba went straight to the kitchen but the others stayed in the rooms where the meal would be served, and worked on setting up the tables and chairs.

Deb was already in full roar when Bathsheba arrived. She had come much earlier in the morning with one of the supervisors to put the last of the turkeys into the ovens. Bathsheba was put on the fruit salad, washing and then slicing apples and pears, and later peeling oranges and grapefruit. The work was straightforward, easy, and Bathsheba relaxed.

Deb's noise became part of the background din, and the smell of burst oranges on Bathsheba's fingers mingled with the richer odor of cooking fowl. Bathsheba felt a mixture of peace and hope, such as she had not felt since she'd stepped into the 1990s a scant month earlier. All of the confusion, all of the many changes . . . all of that faded now and Bathsheba just felt happy in the bustling kitchen, in her small place within it.

Then her arms were forced tight against her sides from behind. It was Deb, and Bathsheba tensed.

"Didn't you hear me, Sunrise?" Deb boomed. "We're just about finished. And we done real good this year, in spite of — we done real good." Deb moved on and back–hugged and slapped or high–fived everyone in the room.

The next hour was busy but not as driven as the earlier kitchen work had been. Bathsheba stood next to Mauri in one of the serving lines, spooning out peas and creamed string beans, concentrating to land them in attractive piles on the plasticized plates. For the most part the food evaded her efforts, partly because she was busy glancing at the guests as they passed in front of her with their plates.

121

They came in more shapes, sizes and colors that Bathsheba could have ever imagined.

Bathsheba had expected them to be sad and shuffling. But they were not. Many were somewhat ill at ease at first, but they were soon chatting convivially with their seat mates. After serving everyone else Bathsheba filled her plate and wedged herself in between a man with a scraggly beard and a large woman who talked a lot about the "projects" where she lived.

"Boy fell down one o' them elevator shafts jus' las' week," the woman was saying. "Broke both his leg — lucky he didn't break his dum head open. That's what his granma say too. Lucky he didn't break his head open. You jus' can't keep dem boys outta dere. Some o' the girls too."

"What er they doin' in there?" the man asked over Bathsheba's head.

"Mischief," the lady snorted back. "Jus' ol' mischief. Don't have enuf else t' do."

"Now I don't believe I'd want to wrestle with a lift," the man said, "even if I didn't have anything better t' do. But as a boy in Sydney there were many times that we'd —"

"Sunrise." It was Deb tapping on Bathsheba's shoulder. "There's a place over there for you. I want you to meet my sister–in–law from Georgia."

Bathsheba's choked on her mashed potatoes. "Oh," she spluttered, "how lovely."

"Yes. Well, come on then."

Bathsheba excused herself and followed Deb with her plate, cup and silverware. When she passed Stan he looked up, and his eyebrows raised in a way that they always did whenever he'd tell her, "You look like you're on your way to the guillotine."

Bathsheba worked hard to rearrange her face into something that she hoped looked less stricken, and within moments she was clutching her dinner in front of a snazzily–dressed brown woman who'd stood up next to an empty chair. The woman said with a wide smile, "Sit down here girl and lemme hear you talk. My name's Gladys, an' I'm just dyin' to hear some o' that good ol' down home sound."

"Er, how do you do?" Bathsheba said softly, self–consciously.

122

Gladys's brow wrinkled slightly and her eyes sharpened, but she swung on pleasantly. "It's like I've been tellin' all these folks up here, that they just don't know how to talk civilized like. Sometimes I just want to stand on the street corner an' yell out for someone to talk Southern to me for a while. So, Sunrise, what part of the Peach State are you from?"

Bathsheba blinked a few times before she realized that Gladys must mean Georgia. "Oh," she mustered nervously, "from a plan–– from a farm near Mirard. Do you, um, do you know that part of Georgia?"

"Mirard? Why, I don't believe I've even heard of Mirard. Is that a real small town, sugar?"

"Oh, yes, it's very, very small," answered Bathsheba, relaxing slightly. "It's near the Savannah River, near Gainesboro."

"Oh. Well, I'm a Savannah gal myself. Ever been there?"

Bathsheba certainly had, but she wasn't about to admit it now. It probably wasn't anything like it had been 140 years ago.

"No," she lied, "I never did get to Savannah. But I've, I've heard it's a real pretty little town."

"Bite your tongue, girl!" Gladys exploded, and Bathsheba tensed up again. "Savannah's a darn tootin' big city!"

"No it ain't, honey," put in a big burly man on the other side of Gladys. He smiled at Bathsheba while Gladys poked him in his side with her elbow. "N'York's big," he continued. "Chicago's big. Los Angeles big. But Savannah, she real small."

"Oh!" Gladys poked him again in mock disgust. "You New York folks are just so spoiled, is all. But for Georgia, Savannah is a big city, and I'm not going to let anybody say otherwise."

Bathsheba had been looking at the big man. "I'll wager you're Deb's brother," she hazarded, desperate to get the conversation away from Georgia.

The big guy smiled. "That's right," he said. "I'm Mike. N'York born and bred. Like Deb."

"And here you are, helping out with this meal, instead of having Thanksgiving in your own home," Bathsheba pressed on.

"Yeah," said Gladys, "the first Thanksgiving I was up here, they all said, 'You got to come help out at the mission.' And I said,

123

'What?! I got to do what?!' But I come that year, and every year since then. Been about five years now, I reckon.

"Now, you were in the kitchen all day yesterday with Deb, weren't you? How was it, then, workin' under that big ol' sweet sister–in–law of mine?" Gladys purred.

"Well, Deb is certainly very assertive," Bathsheba hazarded, and Gladys and her husband turned heads a few tables away with their burst of laughter.

"You said it, sister," Gladys said as soon as she could stop laughing. "Why, when I first come up here I was more afraid of Deb than I was of the subway and the drug dealers, and I was pretty scared of them all right. Why, that Deb's just like a big ol' steam roller when she gets goin'."

Bathsheba smiled faintly and nodded, and again Gladys and Mike burst into laughter.

Bathsheba spoke as little as possible, but whenever she said more than a few words at a time, Gladys's head would cock and her eyes would linger on her. Fortunately for Bathsheba though, Gladys was rather talkative, so it was Bathsheba who ended up experiencing most of the comfort of hearing the sing song and longed out vowels of Georgia again. It wasn't the Georgia twang that she was used to, but it was similar enough to evoke home in taut lurches of nostalgia. It was like a poetry that she'd missed more than she'd realized in the past month, even though it was jarring sometimes, when she didn't recognize a string of words and sounds in Gladys's speech. It was sort of like Gladys was occasionally speaking in a foreign language.

The minutes dragged by for Bathsheba. She dreaded being found out as unauthentic by this lively, friendly woman, and she wondered what Gladys would think if she knew the truth. Bathsheba was only too glad when it was time to serve dessert. She took a place in the serving line beside Mauri again and handed over slices from cakes and pies that had been brought in. She served the Australian and the projects lady among the others, and paid little attention to the buzz of conversation around her until she caught a few words in Gladys's distinctive voice behind her. Mauri was listening too.

"Someone else from the South?" Mauri whispered to Bathsheba.

"From Savannah, Georgia," Bathsheba whispered back. "I had to talk with her at dinner."

124

"Oh–oh," Mauri whispered back, and Bathsheba nodded solemnly.

It was Gladys and Deb behind them, helping with the trash bags for the dinner plates. Gladys apparently didn't realize that Bathsheba was so close by. At least Bathsheba didn't think she'd be talking the way that she was, if she had known.

"It's sure not any Georgia talk that I recognize," Gladys was saying. "It's real thick like, but with an odd sort of pattern to it, a different emphasis. She must be real deep country, Deb. Sort of a cross between the way my ol' granny — why, that's it, Deb. She forms up her words just like some real hick old lady would. And to my ears, it sounds mighty strange coming out of a girl."

"Well, her people was hippies," Deb commented. "Maybe that accounts for it."

"Yeah, well, maybe. Maybe."

Mauri nudged Bathsheba and grinned, but Bathsheba wasn't as reassured.

Mrs. Rodriguez came up to Bathsheba during the general clean up.

"You'll be back tomorrow then," she asked, "to help with the regular meal?"

"Yes," Bathsheba answered.

Mrs. Rodriguez smiled. "Not nearly so many people. And Deb, she here only for the Thanksgiving and the Christmas meal. You know already?"

"I know already," Bathsheba answered, and smiled back. "And thank you for —"

"It's okay. No problems. All fixed," Mrs. Rodriguez asserted with a grin.

Bathsheba left soon afterward with her family. Deb, Gladys and Mike waved to them from across the street on their way to their car. The afternoon was damp and overcast; darkness was already beginning to overhang the streets. But Bathsheba felt contented. She had seen so many people today who had to be down on their luck, maybe had been for a very long time, perhaps for as long as they could remember. But it had so impressed her that they were not morose and shuffling about it, as she had thought they would be. They had become relaxed and convivial over the good meal that she

125

had helped to prepare. She felt good, even elated, by it all. Nothing in her experience had prepared her for the scale and breadth of the mission's charity meal.

And she felt grateful. Mauri, Stan and Mrs. Bale had undertaken to help her, when they didn't really have to. She had much to repay them for, besides her board and the money that they had advanced for her new identity. She would work hard. They would see that she knew how to repay a debt of sincere gratitude. She felt for the first time since entering the 1990s that the world was opening up before her. She was beginning to realize that she had some choices, and she was eager to work to improve them.

"We've got a real treat for you, Theba," Stan announced on the drive home.

"Oh–oh," Bathsheba said, and everybody laughed. That was the line that Stan often used just before they introduced her to something that required a very distinct stretch of her imagination, and a certain amount of guts. Like the time that he and Mauri took Bathsheba on her first subway ride.

"No, really," Stan insisted. "It's something nice. I taped the Macy's Thanksgiving Day Parade, so that we wouldn't miss it."

"Oh?" Theba asked, still not sure if this was a good thing or not.

"This time it's okay, Theba," Mauri reassured her.

They made popcorn and hot cocoa when they got home, and then sat down in front of the tv.

"This is going to be fun," Mauri commented. "I haven't seen the parade in ages." But her voice sounded a little odd, a little tight. Everybody noticed it.

"Your father used to take you two urchins to the parade every year," Mrs. Bale said quietly.

"Yeah, until the time that it rained and our feet nearly froze off," Mauri whispered. "We were getting too old for it by then anyway, I guess."

"Speak for yourself, Sis," Stan said as he slid the rewound tape into the VCR. "I could never get enough of Supertoot, Gumfield and all of those other balloons floating over our heads."

"You're just like Dad," Mauri said.

"Yeah," from Stan, and then the parade, time–shifted by pre–programming, began.

126

Soon they were all in stitches. Stan kept up a patter of explanations for Bathsheba, and Mauri overcame her initial reserve of sadness and joined in gamely.

But then Mauri broke down over the old Gaggles balloon. Up until then, tears had glistened in her eyes, and her voice had wobbled uncharacteristically from time to time. But when the old black–nosed beagle floated onto the tv screen she left the room with tears streaming.

"That's a real old balloon," Stan commented quietly. "Been in the parade for years."

Soon came the Santa float and Mauri slipped back in as soon as the tv announcer's patter signaled that it was past.

"Here comes the best part," Mauri said tightly, tears still on her face. "The street sweepers."

Mauri's mother sat down beside her and put an arm around her shoulders. They all watched as the convoy of the New York City Sanitation Department's finest rumbled down Broadway. The broom–pushers strutted at a smart pace in front of them, shwooshing the debris toward the roaring maws of the big machines.

"Dad used to cheer the sweepers on every year," Mauri whispered through tears. "He yelled louder and wilder for them than he did for anything else in the whole parade." And then she bent her head over her hands and sobbed.

Stan turned the TV off and headed for the kitchen, mumbling about fixing another round of cocoa. Mrs. Bale stroked her daughter's hair, and tears brimmed in Bathsheba's eyes.

"I wish I could have met him," Bathsheba said.

"Yeah," Mauri croaked, fighting for a grip on herself.

"Yeah," echoed Mrs. Bale. "You would have liked him, Theba. Almost everybody liked him. He was a real nut."

"Mom!" Mauri bawled. "He was not! He was just, just . . . well, a little nutty maybe, but not —"

"Hey, I need some help in here," came Stan's voice from the kitchen. "Somebody's, um, hidden the sugar . . . again."

"Oh! I think I put that away," Bathsheba said, hurrying off to the kitchen.

Mauri and Mrs. Bale came into the kitchen while the cocoa was being ladled into the mugs.

Conversation was sporadic and desultory until about halfway through the cocoa. Then Stan glanced at his watch again. Bathsheba had noticed him doing that several times during the parade and in the kitchen. Much more often than usual.

"My dear family — ah, including you, Theba," Stan said portentously. "I think I've got a — ahem, a treat for you."

Silence. His audience just stared at him and Stan — uncharacteristically — kept his eyes fixed on the cocoa in his mug.

"Oh—oh," Theba said softly, but this time nobody laughed. There was something in Stan's deliberate avoidance of their eyes that gave them pause.

"Oh?" asked Mrs. Bale at last. "What is it, Stan?"

"It's Zekial," Stan announced.

"Zekial," Mrs. Bale stated. "What about Zekial?" she prompted.

"He's coming here. Nine o'clock flight into LaGuardia. With Prentis. I have to leave in about ten minutes to go and pick them up."

"They're coming here?" Mauri asked stupidly.

"Yes," answered Stan. "Prentis has to go back on Saturday, but Zekial is going to have to, ah, stay for an, um, a month or so."

"Stay?" Mrs. Bale asked, still calm, but her voice was hardening. "Here?"

"He can share my room. And I'll, I'll take care of him, Mom."

"Stan, you've got finals in two weeks."

"I'll manage, Mom. It'll be fine."

And then Stan explained. Rapidly, fiddling with the car keys and the ear of his cocoa mug. He had called Prentis last weekend to ask how Zekial was doing. Prentis had been about to call him. Zekial wasn't doing too well. Nobody had enough time to work with him, and he needed lots of help. Prentis couldn't take him to stay at the University with him until January at the earliest, when one of his roommates was moving out. And his dad was going into the hospital on the Monday after Thanksgiving for bypass surgery. Prentis was going to shuttle back and forth between the University and Mirard to help his mom with the motel, which was getting busy with holiday travelers.

And on top of everything else, Officer Welson had been around several times, wanting to ask Zekial questions. Each time they had just barely managed to evade the pesky officer.

"So this is only for a month," Mrs. Bale stated when Stan finished.

"Thanks, Mom," Stan said and hugged and kissed her. But Mrs. Bale pushed him off.

"You brat!" she said to him. "Why didn't you tell us sooner?"

"Well, Prentis and I didn't actually settle on it all until Tuesday evening."

"You know that's not what I meant."

Stan was at the back door. "Yeah, I know, Mom," he said. "It's just that, well, you haven't met Zekial yet. And I think of him as, as sort of my . . . responsibility. Through, through Dad — I mean, Dad's family. I mean, he was their slave and all. I had to do it. And I knew you weren't going to be . . . pleased, so I decided to, to . . ."

"Spring it on me," Mrs. Bale finished for him grimly.

"Yes," Stan admitted. "But it'll all work out okay. I'm sure it will. But I've got to go now. Got to meet their flight."

Mrs. Bale didn't say anything, and Stan took that as his signal to leave.

"Mom," Mauri asked, "will you need me to help with the linens and such?" Mauri asked.

"No, no," Mrs. Bale said, irked but capable. "You go on with Stan, Mauri. You, too, Theba, if you want to."

Bathsheba wanted to. She wanted to be there when Zekial got off the plane. She wanted to help him over the next month. She knew his mind better than the others. Maybe she could help him a lot.

She smiled at Zekial when he saw her standing next to Stan and Mauri by the gate, but Zekial did not smile back. Bathsheba rearranged her face quickly as her excitement and fine plans to help him along faded. She knew even before Zekial spoke that he was angry, and that his anger was directed squarely at her.

"Howdy, Stannie," Zekial said evenly. "An' Mauri. Hallo."

"But Stannie," he added, "what dat white bish doin' hea?"

Chapter 11

The little white pony blipped madly across the screen.

"Not dat way, yu dum hoss," Zekial grumbled. "Yu done gone too far dat way."

"Zekial," Stan put in, using his most soothing voice, "you have to lift your finger off the arrow key or else the pony will just to keep going in that direction, to the far side of the screen."

Zekial looked down and seemed surprised to discover his finger still down on the key.

"Oh," he said, lifting it off.

"Maybe if you try tapping at the key, instead of holding it down. Like this." Stan demonstrated a light touch. "Now you try it."

Zekial did, and he got it to work a little better. He lined up the pony under the picture that matched the three–letter word in the pony's pen. He pressed the enter key and the computer chirped, "Yeeesssss! Hooray for you! Giddyup!"

But Zekial looked unwilling, and discouraged.

"What's the matter, Zekial?" Stan asked.

"Nothin'."

"Maybe you're a little tired."

"Mmm, mebbe." Zekial went silent and Stan waited. Zekial did things like this one step at a time. And there was no point in continuing with Reading Pony until whatever was bothering him was out and dealt with.

"It dis here hoss," Zekial finally said.

"Oh? What's the matter with it, Zekial?"

"Ain't a proper hoss, Stannie. Ain't no hoss got a gait like dat," and Zekial pressed the other arrow key to make the little pony scurry back across the screen.

Stan knew that the pony's gait wasn't the problem though. Zekial loved cartoons, especially the Tasmanian Devil and Daffy Duck, and

130

neither of them moved like real animals. The pony on the screen was bothering him, but it wasn't the gait. Stan waited some more.

"An' he white, Stannie. I don't like dis hoss cuz he a white 'un. He look white, an' he *talk* white."

"Whew," Stan said, "I wish that I could change the pony's color and the way he talks, Zekial. That kind of stuff still bothers me too, sometimes. But they probably made him white so he'd show up better on the screen — just so that he'd be easier to see. And the voice is really sort of accentless, that's all. A black person could talk that way as well as a white one could."

Zekial shook his head adamantly. "Das white talk, Stannie. It jus ain't natural for' a Af'can Mercan hoss t' talk dat way."

Stan didn't try to argue the point. He just jotted down a note to himself to find some videotapes of African Americans talking — like Dr. King's speeches and such.

"We can turn the sound off if you don't want to hear the voice," Stan suggested. "And I'll try to find another reading program that's more . . . acceptable. In the meantime, do you think that you could put up with this white pony for a little while longer?"

Zekial turned from the computer screen and faced Stan glumly. "I be a lot o' trouble fo' yu," Zekial began, and Stan groaned.

"Zekial, please, let's not go over that again. We're really *glad* you're here. We like you very much. And you're doin' a great job with learning to read and write. You really are."

"In de lib'ry wid Mauri las' evenin', dis lil' bitty gal readin' much better'n me," Zekial groused. "An' I axe her how many year she got, an' she say fo'. She fo' year, Stannie, an' she readin' better'n me."

"That's probably because she's been exposed to it probably since she was about two years old, or maybe even before that," Stan rejoined. "You'd have read that well at four years old if you'd had the same chance at it."

"Tink so?"

"I know it," Stan lied — not because Zekial wasn't smart enough to have read well at age four. Stan just thought that Zekial probably would have been more interested in other things than reading at that age. "That little girl has probably had bedtime stories read to her from age one or two years old," Stan continued. "And she's probably also had picture books from the library all the time, and words and

131

pictures all over the walls at her preschool . . . and, um, computer programs like this one to make learning even more, um, fun."

Zekial turned back to the computer screen scowling and Stan, watching him turn away, had a sudden inspiration.

"Tell me some more about this little girl at the library," he asked Zekial. "Was she cute?"

"Cute?" Zekial asked, turning back to Stan.

"Pretty. Attractive."

"Oh. Yeah, she real cute, Stannie. She got this big smile. Real big smile, like dis." Zekial spread his arms wide and smiled big too.

"You're gonna have a cute little girl like that one someday, Zekial."

Zekial's arms flopped down and his smile disappeared.

"I already done got me —"

"I know, I know. But I mean a twentieth century little girl, Zekial. Or a twenty–first century girl. Boys too. Don't ask me how I know, but I just know it."

Zekial shook his head, but he smiled a little bit.

"Now," Stan continued, "if you want your little girl to read when she's four, you're gonna have to start reading to her when she's one and two years old. Bedtime stories. Every night."

Zekial shook his head again. "Ma woman'll do dat," he said. "Dem lil' gals o' mine, dere ma'll read to 'em. Dere ma'll already know all dis readin' stuff."

"Zekial!" said Stan, as if he was shocked. "I'm 'shamed o' you, boy. Twentieth century women'll only read to 'em *half* the time. For the other half, it's your turn."

"Nah," Zekial said, but he half–snorted, half–laughed.

"Ain't no nineteenth century women 'round here for you," Stan continued, shaking his head mournfully.

"Aw, Stannie —"

"And before the women are going to be interested in you, they're going to expect you to be able to read, Zekial."

"Even Mauri?" Zekial asked suddenly, and kind of shy.

"Mauri?!" Stan asked, really surprised.

"Yeah," Zekial replied simply. "Mauri."

When Stan didn't say anything Zekial continued. "I be thinkin' a lot about Mauri, Stannie. I be thinkin' she a real fine gal."

Stan blinked and tried to consider Zekial and Mauri . . . but it couldn't work, he thought. Or could it? He determined to check with Mauri about it. Meantime he'd have to be careful to neither encourage nor discourage Zekial.

"Well," he said, "in any case, Zekial, reading is something you'll need to be able to do. And you're doing real well at it. It'll speed up once you get the basics down. The, um, pony part."

"Umph," Zekial said with a frown.

"Let's take a break, Zekial," Stan suggested, even though they were already in the middle of one. "You've been at this for a while."

Zekial thought for a minute, staring off into space. Then, "No, Stannie," he said, turning back to the computer.

"No?"

"I got to wrassle some wi' dis here dam white hoss."

"Ah, want me to turn the sound off for you, Zekial?"

"Nope."

Zekial tapped the arrow key until the pony was under the picture matching the next corralled word, and pressed the enter key. "You are such a smart little cowpoke!" the computer trilled.

"Shut up yu dam white rascul," Zekial told it, and began to tap the pony over to the next match.

* * *

"I don't care how much you dislike Bathsheba," Mrs. Bale told Zekial that evening, "I will not have you muttering insults at her every time your paths cross in this house."

"But she *is* a white bish," Zekial countered, "an', an' all o' dem udder tings." But his voice lacked the complete conviction required to carry his point. It wasn't because he didn't believe that he was right about Bathsheba. It was because of the way that Mrs. Bale looked and sounded right now: a force that many stronger than Zekial would be inclined to give way to. And just in the space of a week in her household, Zekial had learned that she was very shrewd about choosing her fights, and that as a result she lost very few of them.

She was definitely in full battle form now, and she had timed this particular contest well: she was still in her nurse's uniform and dinner was almost ready. She knew that her uniform impressed Zekial, and she also knew how much he hated to be in any kind of turmoil while he ate. Standing there in the kitchen with Mauri, Stan and Bathsheba close by, she and Zekial already knew that he was going to have to capitulate. It was only a matter of how much face Mrs. Bale was going to allow him to save.

"Does anybody else in this household call Bathsheba a bitch, or any of those other things?" Mrs. Bale asked.

No one spoke.

"And even if she is what you call her, Zekial," Mrs. Bale swept on, "she's shown no signs of it while she's been here with us. Therefore I think that she's earned the right to be left alone about it. You've expressed your opinion of her: we all know your viewpoint. Now it's time for you to start keeping that opinion to yourself around here, out of respect for the rest of us, if for no other reason."

Zekial recognized the peace branch that Mrs. Bale was holding out to him, and he seized it.

"Thas right," he said. "I haf great deal o' respect fo' de res' o' yu — fo' ever'body 'cept dat white — fo' ever'body 'cept dat white womun."

"Then we can all eat," Mrs. Bale stated. "In peace."

"Yes'm," Zekial felt impelled to reply.

Later that evening Stan asked Mauri to go with him on a grocery run. When they were in the car Stan got right to the point.

"How much to you like Zekial, Mauri?"

"Ah, Zekial?"

"Yep."

"Talk English, Bro."

"He's sweet on you, Mauri."

"Did he tell you that?"

"Something very close to it, Sis. You notice it already?"

"Well, I suppose I was beginning to wonder."

"Well?"

"Well, what?"

"Well, do you like him back?"

Mauri was silent for a while. When she spoke it was toward the windshield. "He's got so much to learn, and what he wants for himself is bound to change a lot in the next year or so," she said carefully.

134

"I notice that you didn't answer my question."

"Oh, he's okay. He's more than okay."

"My, aren't we detached," Stan commented drily. "Is it possible that we're sweet on somebody else?"

"Mmm . . . it's possible."

"A–ha! Somebody at work probably."

"S'possible."

"Well, who?"

But Mauri shook her head.

"Well, whatever you do, don't confide in little ol' me, your very favorite brother in the whole world."

Mauri smiled. "Seems to me you've got plenty of other things to worry yourself about right now. Finals next week . . . your part of Bathsheba's G.E.D. preparation, and last but not least, the bulk of Zekial's education and acculturation."

"Besides," she added, "it's early yet, Bro. Way too early to even mention it at home."

"Okay. Okay. It looks like I'll just have to wait on that. But in the meantime, what about Zekial?"

Mauri thought about it for a few minutes. "I don't want to hurt his feelings," she then said. "But at the same time, he shouldn't have unrealistic expectations. And besides, he'll be going back to Georgia in January."

"Dreams are powerful motivators," Stan commented, thinking about the little girl at the library.

"Yes, Professor Stan."

"Well, let me know if you need help with it."

"Alright, if you let me know if you need help with, um, with Theba."

"With who?!"

"You heard me."

"I don't know what you're talking about, Sis."

"Liar."

* * *

Several days later Mauri needed the help with Zekial that Stan had offered, but Stan wasn't there. Neither was her mom or even Theba.

Zekial was sitting next to Mauri on the living room couch.

"An' so I wuz wonderin', Mauri, what yu really tink o' me."

Mauri's palms started sweating. Every day Zekial veered between 1859 and the 1990s, often several times and sometimes with wrenching abruptness. Everyone else — including Bathsheba, whom Zekial was now coldly ignoring — tried to track his state of mind and to keep him in the 1990s.

"He's not with us this morning," Stan would mention over their hasty breakfast before Mauri and Bathsheba left for their commutes. "I can tell by the way he's mumbling, "I do it. I do it in a minut Massa John. Comin' right 'way."

Zekial's 1990s mode was a general hopefulness, but it was undercut by bewilderment and uncertainty. He could not fully believe in the 1990s yet. His natural confidence in himself was broad, but his slave upbringing had rendered it eggshell thin.

His 1859 mode developed into a heavy lassitude, bordering on despair.

It was the inbetween states, however, which were of increasing concern to the others in the household. Then Zekial would seem to completely lose track of himself and do disturbing things. Like spasming similar to his state when Officer Welson had been staring him, back in Georgia. Or muttering phrases to himself, over and over, in a distracted way. "De gal w' de — read! Read, yu dum nigger! Read, dam you!" Or, "I'se a comin', comin', comin', I'se a comin', comin', comin'. Dam yo' white ase! I'se a comin' yo' white ase!"

Stan had told Bathsheba and Mauri at breakfast this morning that yesterday Zekial had begun hitting the side of his head — hard, relentless —when he'd had trouble with a new part of the math program.

"Time to ease off, Bro," Mauri had said.

"Yeah," Stan agreed. "I'm gonna let him sleep in this morning, and then we'll go on one of our history talking walks. That ought to cheer him up a little."

"Did you ever have time to find him a different computer program for reading?" Bathsheba asked.

"No," Stan replied and buried his nose in his molecular biology notes. Mauri and Bathsheba left for the city soon afterward.

136

This was the day of the week when Bathsheba went to the library after her work at the soup kitchen, so Mauri had expected only Stan and Zekial to be at home when she arrived there after work. But Stan wasn't there, and Zekial told her that after their history walk Stan had gone to pick up some class notes from a friend, while Zekial had begged off with a headache.

But he didn't seem to have a headache now, and he seemed pleased to have a chance to talk with Mauri alone. He was agitated — spasming faintly, but he also, in fits and starts, glanced at Mauri and smiled as if elated. Or infatuated. Vacillating, Mauri guessed nervously. Highly volatile. She braced herself.

"I think you're a very friendly guy, Zekial," she answered him. "That's what I really tink — think — of you."

Zekial quieted his restless limbs then and looked straight at Mauri.

"I mean, I mean as a man, Mauri," he said, "as a, a man."

Mauri knew that Zekial was sincere. And his bearing had considerable dignity, all the more amazing for coming from someone floundering, and torn–up–inside.

"That was beautiful, Zekial," Mauri said softly, almost mesmerized by his undiluted need to be loved as a man.

"Whut wuz?" he asked with confusion wrinkling his brow. "Whut wuz beau – ti – ful?" he asked with the precision of intense curiosity.

Mauri had a powerful feeling of being drawn to Zekial, but when she smiled at him again it was with relief. Zekial's confusion had broken his unconscious, momentary spell.

Zekial stared at the smiling girl and his love for her deepened many fold. He already admired her. He was already attracted to her, and now he was sure that she would not deliberately hurt him.

Mauri was casting about for something to say when they both heard the front door open. Stan, they both thought. They stayed seated next to each other, watching the room's doorway, as the footsteps came down the hall carpet. Then Bathsheba stood at the room's threshold.

Zekial fists clenched and he hunched forward. "Go 'way!" he snarled at Bathsheba, "Go 'way yu white —"

137

Mauri put her hand on Zekial's arm. "Zekial," she said quickly, "remember what my mother said."

Zekial swung his face to Mauri's and then looked down at her hand on his arm. Mauri saw him swallowing his hatred, forcing it down even though it was almost too difficult.

"I do it," he told her, shuddering, "I do it out o' respec' fo' you, Mauri. Out o' respec' fo' you an' not dat —," and he turned to glare at Bathsheba in the doorway. But she was no longer there.

*　*　*

"I bought it for Zekial," Bathsheba told Mauri later that evening. "And I'd like for you to give it to Stan for him. Don't tell either of them that it's from me."

Mauri looked at the box that Bathsheba was holding out.

"Reading Wizard," was emblazoned across it, with lightning flashes and swirls of blue smoke around the words. "Playful, painless learning while your child helps the Wizard Shazeemo defeat the Evil Word Stiflers," she read in some smaller print. "Ages 4 to —"

"Theba," Mauri asked, "where did you get this?"

"Well, I've been walking to the mission instead of taking the subway and the bus."

"But that's sixty blocks!"

Bathsheba shrugged. "Sometimes I just don't fancy riding in those underground trains," she said. "And there is a store for computers that I pass every day —"

"Every day. You mean you walk there every day?"

"Well, most days," Bathsheba admitted.

"But how did you know what kind of program to get? And how did you, um, pay for it?"

"The salesman helped me. He told me what to look for on Stan's computer. And I paid for it mostly with the subway fare that I've been saving."

"Theba, this is just . . . unreal."

"Oh?" Bathsheba frowned.

"Er, it's just an expression. It means that this is, this is very surprising."

Bathsheba shrugged uncomfortably. "I think we were all getting tired of that 'dam white hoss'," she said. "And this wizard can be

138

either male or female, and you can adjust its skin, um, tone. But, um, well, the salesman ran it for me on a store computer and . . . I'm afraid that the voice is going to sound white to Zekial."

Mauri smiled at the genuinely worrying eyes of her triple–great aunt. "The voice'll be okay," she said. "Stan's been having Zekial listen to some of Dr. King's speeches, and Zekial has even started to — but Theba, I don't want to take the credit for this."

"You have to," Bathsheba replied matter–of–factly. "Zekial won't even look at it if he knows it's from me."

"And Stan?" Mauri asked. "Why shouldn't Stan know?"

Bathsheba looked at Mauri steadily. "I think you know why," she replied.

Mauri glanced away to the Reading Wizard box.

"I like your brother a lot," Bathsheba continued, "a lot more, I think, than he'll ever like me. So it's . . . awkward, and my getting this program is only likely to, to . . ."

"Both you and Zekial are in transition," Mauri began.

"That," Bathsheba interrupted, "is an understatement. Yes, a lot is going to change. And I, I — excuse me," Bathsheba blurted and left the bedroom suddenly. Mauri found a note stuck to the fridge when she went into the kitchen to check on the casserole in the oven. "Gone for a walk," it said in Bathsheba's quaint handwriting.

Mauri's mother arrived home while Mauri was putting the peas into a pot. "Can I talk to you later, Mom?" Mauri asked her.

"Oh? What about Mauri?" asked Mrs. Bale, taking off her coat.

"Love trouble," Mauri replied, putting a lid onto the pot.

"9:30, my room."

"Thanks."

* * *

"I done beat Level Three today, Mauri," Zekial said, shy and yet proud.

"Level Three!"

"Yes'm — that is, yes. I'm gettin' ahead with that there Wizard Shazeemo."

"That's really great, Zekial."

139

"Yep." Zekial sighed with happiness. This had become his favorite time of the week. The library was open until nine o'clock on Thursdays, and he was on his way there with Mauri.

It was very cold. A dusting of icy snow crunched under his feet. But from head to toe he was well–insulated from the weather. A lined fisherman's hat, a heavy scarf wrapped around his nose and mouth, a down jacket, long johns under his jeans, thick mittens and socks, and fine pair of supple hunting boots.

Zekial loved all of his new clothes, even the underwear which took some getting used to. He had spent hours with Stan in the stores picking out the items one by one. Slowly he had fingered every seam and smoothed every panel of each article of clothing, with profound absorption. He asked Stan and the sales clerk many questions that they couldn't answer — innumerable comparative questions of quality and cut. He wore out most of the sales clerks: they would usually abandon him and Stan after the first twenty minutes or so of his idiosyncratic rummaging among their racks. Those few clerks who remained patiently faithful and attentive were those who had the time and inclination to marvel over this strange– talking customer who took the selection of his clothing so very seriously. "I'm so glad you were able to select these socks without having to convene a summit meeting," one of them once quipped wearily.

Zekial listened to the daily weather forecasts with a similar avidity, and minutely compared the forecasts against the actual atmospheric conditions by going constantly to the backdoor to check their accuracy. Then whenever it was time to go out he would contemplate which combination of outerwear to don with intense seriousness. Was it too warm for long johns? Was it cold enough for thick socks and boots, or would regular socks and sneakers do? And he was always quietly pleased when his careful work paid off and he was comfortably attired for the day.

Today that quiet pleasure added to the happiness of the library trip. The sky was dark, the icy snow crunched, but he was comfortable and Mauri was by his side. His happiness was expansive and near overflowing.

"I wish that Stannie not have t' be studyin' so," he commented, wishing that his friend could be similarly carefree and happy.

140

"It'll soon be over," Mauri soothed.

"But he actin' plum strange," Zekial confided. "He near jump out of his skin when I done axe him if he think it be cole enuf for the long johnnies. His eyes go plum wild."

"Yeah. Nerves," Mauri said smiling. "You should have seen me the evening before the C.P.A. exam. Stan had a friend over and they accidentally set off the smoke alarm with some popcorn that they burned. The noise and the burning smell just got to me. I came roaring out of my room, grabbed a broom and chased them both out of the house with it, screaming my head off at them."

"No!"

"Yes. I must have looked and sounded pretty wild, because they sure ran fast when they got out the door. Jerry peeled off at his grandmother's house, but I chased Stan all the way down to Elber's Park.

"All the way down there?!"

"Yeah. And to this day Jerry never comes over when I'm around. Stan has to go over there. The kind of sad part is that they were trying to make the popcorn for me."

"What happen when you got down to the park?"

"I chased Stan around the duck pond for a while and then just sat down on a bench and stared into space. Stan jogged home and got . . . he got Dad. He came for me in the car. We sat in the car for a long while, talking . . . about things."

Mauri and Zekial were silent for a while. Then Mauri said, "You would have liked my Dad, Zekial. Even though he was a white guy."

Zekial didn't answer, but his mood darkened somewhat. "I don' unnerstan'," he said softly, "why yo' mama done marry herself a white, a white . . ."

"Well, she did. And I wouldn't be who I am if she hadn't."

"Hummsph," was Zekial's unhappy reply.

"Are you still miffed with my mother about the —"

"Mif? Mif? I ain't no mif," Zekial asserted. "She done talk like a mama su'pose t' talk — these here days anyways — t' somebody sweet on her gal. But it this char'ty work she axe me t' do, this dinner nex week that I su'pose t' do with that white . . . that white . . ."

141

"There'll be a lot of other people there, Zekial," Mauri said, "working on the mission's Christmas dinner. Not just Bathsheba. And the rest of us will be there the next day to help serve it.

"It's really the most practical charity work that she could think of," Mauri continued. "You two could look out for each other —"

"Never! I never do no look out for that white —"

"Please don't be so quick about it, Zekial. You don't know what might come up. Just try to keep an open mind." Mauri stopped there. She sensed that she had pressed it as far as Zekial could stand right now. He was usually more receptive on these weekly library trips, but white people — and particularly Bathsheba — was a sore subject with him even under the best of circumstances.

He had been coming along amazingly, especially after Stan had shown him the video of Martin Luther King's "I have a dream" speech, from 1963. He embraced some parts of the man and his speech wholeheartedly, listening to it over and over again, and he was trying, when he wasn't overly excited, to form his words in the same way as Dr. King. But the parts of the speech about getting along with whites — it was simply too soon for him.

"I wonder if that little girl will be at the library tonight," Mauri soothed as they went up the library steps.

Zekial's mood lightened again. Light spilled out of every window of the large building, catching in the snow crystals in Mauri's hair and on her woolen hat. Zekial looked at her fondly.

"That would be nice," he said as they got to the door.

The little girl was there and Mauri and the girl's father both backed off while the girl and Zekial poured over "Owl At Home" together.

"An' what that word there?" Zekial asked the girl, pointing to the word 'home' in the book.

"Don't you know what that word is?" the girl asked Zekial.

"Well . . . sure I do," Zekial replied uncertainly. And then he grinned down at her. "I jus' testin' t' see if you knows it."

The girl looked at him solemnly for a moment and then looked down at the book.

"It says 'school'," she lied.

Zekial looked at the word and frowned. "You sure?" he asked her. And then they both giggled — quietly, since they were in the

142

library. But sweetly. The child's high musical notes against Zekial's rumbling bass.

Then Zekial suddenly stopped, bringing his sleeve up to his eyes and blinking. The girl stared at him for a moment, wondering what was wrong, and then turned back to the book.

"Okay," she ordered in a crisp whisper. "Let's get to work. I got to go *home* soon. Now you read this part to me. But leave the big words for me 'cause I need the practice. Okay?"

"Yes'm — yep, yes," Zekial replied, recovering himself. He began, "Ol Owl, he wuz at, at . . ."

"Home," the little girl put in.

"How good it . . ."

"Feels."

"My oh my how good it feel t' be, t' be . . ."

"Sitting."

"T' be sittin' by this . . ."

"Fire."

"'By this hea fire,' said Owl," Zekial read.

Zekial was silent for most of the walk home. He was thinking a lot about the girl at the library, and about how much he wanted a child like her of his own, for reading to and for all the other things that having and raising a child meant. In his mind he could see the house that they would have: it was similar to the Bale's house, only much smaller, less spread out. He didn't need such a big place; he preferred to be close in with his woman and children.

In his mind his woman was Mauri — darker skinned somehow, and without her quiet restraint. He saw her more exuberant, sassier, barefoot in their little kitchen, her belly great with another child under a nubby cotton shift. She would be laughing at their eldest boy's prattle while she microwaved the potatoes for their dinner. In his mind he and his little daughter arrived home from the library, both of them laden with books. The little boy would run to the door when they opened it, laughing, shouting, "Poppie! Poppie! You's home! You's home! Gimme five!"

"Les read all these hea books, Poppie," his sturdy laughing daughter would say. Bumped by her little brother, her cornucopia of books would spill out of her arms into a rich profusion around the three of them. They would giggle so much as they picked the books

143

up. "This one! This one!" his daughter would squeal. "No! This one!" his boy would counter and they would all laugh again.

"What's so funny, Zekial?" Mauri asked, and Zekial returned to the present from the hoped–for future.

"Mmm? Oh, nuthin'," was all he could reply with a sappy grin. "Nuthin'."

They walked up the driveway and into the kitchen, where Mrs. Bale and Bathsheba were, with their heads bent over the vegetables for the salad, and their hands working their knife blades along the contours of cucumbers and through some tomatoes. They barely glanced up when Mauri and Zekial came in. 'They are uncommonly attentive to preparing the vegetables,' Mauri thought. 'So grave. Absorbed.' Zekial stood watching them too, sensing also that something was odd about this, but not yet knowing what it was.

A frenzy of excited yells and shouts burst from the direction of Stan and Zekial's room, but the two faces over the vegetables gave no sign of having heard the commotion. Bingo. Mauri and Zekial unanimously headed for the bedroom that Stan and Zekial shared.

As they reached the room they heard Wizard Shazeemo's voice booming from the computer.

"My illustrious assistant, you have saved me once again from the most Evil Word Snitcher of them all! Would you like to play again?"

"Yes! Yes!" Stan boomed back at the computer. "Yes, oh most glorious one, oh King among all Wizards." Stan sprung from his chair, bowed with a deep flourish before the computer monitor and pumped his arms wildly. He threw his head back. "It will be such an enormous thrill to save you once again from the Evil — never fear, Oh Great One, I shall —"

"Stannie," Zekial began.

Stan swung toward the door. "Oh," he said in something more like his usual voice, though his eyes were . . . strange. "Don't worry, Zekial. I started a different file. Your place in Level 3 is intact."

Mauri went back down the hall to the kitchen and propped open the back door. After studying the terrain she grabbed the broom from its hook and said, "Gangway," to the two silent vegetable parers, on her way back through the kitchen.

When she reached Stan and Zekial's room, Stan was pointing at the monitor and excitedly talking to Zekial.

144

". . . and I found this really neat little short cut through the Den of False Crystals to the —"

Mauri leaned the broom against the doorframe, where Stan would see it when he turned around. Then she went to the wall, pulled the computer's plug out, and retreated quickly to the hallway.

"Hey!" shouted Stan, swinging around in his chair.

"Can't catch me!" Mauri sang from the hall, and made a dash for the kitchen. Stan grabbed the broom and was right after her.

"Mauri! Stannie!" Zekial yelled after them. "What yu doin'?! Where yu goin'?!" He jogged into the kitchen, but they were gone by the time he got there. Only the unperturbable Mrs. Bale and Bathsheba were there, silently emptying the sliced vegetables into the wooden salad bowl with the lettuce.

"Hey! Wait for me!" Zekial shouted out the back door, and he ran down the driveway. The block was empty. He thought for a moment and then he began to jog toward Elber's Park.

In his mind he jogged more slowly, with his girl and his boy — a little older now — running at his heels, trying to keep up with their old man. Grinning, laughing, running at his heels.

Chapter 12

"Zekial, this is Mrs. Rodriguez," Bathsheba said.

"I be wanting make one thing full clear," Zekial announced to the short little supervisor at the mission kitchen on Christmas Eve. "I ain't no fren' o' this hea white gal."

Zekial's voice was loud enough for most of the people in the kitchen to hear him, including Deb. There was a momentary lull in the kitchen buzz.

Mrs. Rodriguez's eyes zipped up and down Zekial and to Bathsheba and back again. "We don't have to love each other to work together here," she said to Zekial and Bathsheba. "But we must show each other the respect. Yes?"

Zekial nodded, satisfied. He knew he had gotten his point across to everyone here.

He, Deb and Bathsheba started on the potatoes.

"Mm, mm. I sure do like the smell of a fresh ham baking for Christmas dinner," Deb hazarded to her two glum and silent assistants. "Better 'n turkey. 'Course, us Muslims don't eat ham but I still remember . . . a great big ol' ham, with a thick orange glaze an' . . . oh, so, so good. What about you, Zekial? You usually have ham, or turkey?"

Zekial whittled solemnly at his potato before answering.

"Befo' this hea Christmas, if'n we be wantin' for t' eat ham, other than the head, we haf t' steal us a hog," he then said, glancing darkly at Bathsheba. "We kill 'un and bury 'im in the woods. Cook 'im on the sly, when the wind right. An' if'n we get caught, we gets whipped. Twenty lash. An ever'body pointin' the fingah at ever'body else, sayin' 'That one done it. T'warn't me.'

"No, ma'am. No Christmas ham a'tall. Fo' Christmas the men get a single dram o' whiskey."

"One each," he added distinctly as he tossed his mangled potato into the tub.

146

He was staring hard at Bathsheba, and Deb looked at both of them, frowning with consternation.

When Zekial left off staring at Bathsheba and began to whittle on another potato, Deb asked him, casual like, "Ah, where you from, Zekial?"

"Georgia," Zekial answered grimly. "Ol' Georgia. Same place as this hea . . . whitey."

"S'zat so?" Deb asked, fascinated.

"That's so," Zekial replied. "I ain't got no reason to lie 'bout *my* past." He shook his head violently. "We baun right nex t' the other. 'Course, she bawn in the big house, into a big ol' comfy bed, I reckon. An' I bawn, I bawn in the cabin, on the dirt o' the floor. An' I done seen mos' o' my brudders and sisters bawn the same way, the same way."

Silence. Then, "How many brother and sisters you got, Zekial?" Deb asked.

"Don' matter," Zekial said, slicing his potato into bits, heedlessly, his eyes fixed with hatred on Bathsheba. "They all gone anyway."

"Ah, gone?" Deb asked.

"Sol," Zekial said, his voice shaking. "Sol."

"I, um, don't understand you, Zekial," Deb said blinking, wary. "What's this about their souls?"

"He means they were sold," Bathsheba said quietly. Her voice was even but she did not lift her face from her potato. "My father sold them all to . . . to other whites."

"Sold?!" Deb asked. "Your father . . . what on *earth* are you two talkin' about?"

The potatoes were forgotten. Zekial stared fixedly at Bathsheba, and Deb looked back and forth between them. Finally Bathsheba spoke.

"Zekial and I got sent here from the year 1859," Bathsheba told Deb. "We arrived about two months ago, through some kind of magic done by one of the other . . . slaves. We can't go back — I'm not sure that we'd want to anyway."

Deb stared at Bathsheba. "You jivin' me," she said, incredulous.

Bathsheba didn't answer. Deb turned toward Zekial.

"She jivin' me," she said.

Zekial shook his head and laid his paring knife aside. "You got t' put me on one end o' this hea kitchen, and you got t' put this hea white bish on the udder end. Else I got to leave hea. I can't stay."

Deb blinked. And blinked again.

"Why don't you two stay here?" Bathsheba suggested. "I'll go — I'll find something else to do. And Bathsheba left them before either spoke.

After a few minutes Deb picked up her knife and potato. "Why don't you jus' start at the beginning, Zekial?" she asked him slowly, worriedly.

Bathsheba went to the batter mixer near Mrs. Rodriguez's office. She felt safer there, safer from the past. She tried to pretend that it was just another day at the mission's kitchen. It wasn't, of course. Besides the big, special Christmas dinner that was being prepared for the next day, Zekial was there telling Deb . . . telling Deb everything. Including, she was sure, about the time that she had whipped the slave at the landing. Her aunt had encouraged her to think of that as the capstone of her training. Now she writhed inside about it. Her right hand spasmed. She remembered the feel of her aunt's whip in her hand. She remembered the look of the flesh she had torn and bled with the whip, and the eyes of everyone watching her — all of the yard and the stable slaves, the farmer who'd lost his grain, Buddy and the Meyers boys, and her aunt dominating it all like the wrath of God incarnate.

Bathsheba wondered what Deb would think, what Deb would do. She had made a kind of peace with Deb during the Thanksgiving dinner's preparations. But that was before Deb . . . knew who she really was.

Bathsheba worked steadily but kept a constant check on Deb and Zekial at the other end of the long room. She sensed that it was time for Deb to go into high gear over the dinner preparations: everyone was working, but they were also waiting for Deb. Waiting for Deb's voice to begin its boom at their backs, waiting for Deb's push. Sue made a few attempts to raise the pace, but without Deb bustling and hollering nearby she was too hesitant. Another quarter hour passed. A half hour. Forty–five minutes. And then Deb and Zekial left the potatoes together and came to the center of the room.

148

Deb stared around the kitchen like she had never seen it before. Bathsheba edged closer to where Mrs. Rodriguez stood, both of them watching Deb.

Sue approached Deb and asked her something about the soup stock. Deb blinked several times.

"Deb, you all right?" Sue asked her.

"Hm? Oh. Yeah, yeah. I fine. Fine. I jus' thinkin' hard on somethin'."

"Well, are we gonna get this dinner done or not? That's what *I've* been thinkin' on."

"Oh? Oh, yeah." Deb shook herself. "We gonna do that. We'd better do that . . . now." She gathered herself together. She took another long look at Zekial, and a quick dark look at Bathsheba. And then she filled her lungs with air and commenced.

"Alright I need Stacey n' Janice to finish off them potatoes. We gonna haf' ta mash some of 'em — they's a godawful mess. An' how's that pineapple savory comin' — an' that's no way to stir in that flour! Zekial, you go with Martha here and bring in all the yams for baking."

Her voice gained strength as she continued, but it never reached the crescendo that it had achieved and maintained during the preparations for the Thanksgiving meal. Sue filled in as much of the gap as she could, and Bathsheba surreptitiously saved the dinner once or twice by a timely question about a crucial step in the process. Deb was still the hub of the great kitchen wheel, but the spokes bore more of the axle's weight as the it labored on through the meal's preparations.

The afternoon wore away into early evening, and then the preparations wound down for the night. Bathsheba called the house about a half hour before they finished, and waited just outside the door like she had on Thanksgiving Eve. Stan or Mauri would pick her and Zekial up. Zekial waited across the sidewalk from her, making it perfectly clear that they were not friends.

Deb came out. Bathsheba nodded toward her, and Deb looked from Bathsheba to Zekial.

"It's still kinda hard to believe," she said. "But, but . . . an' did you really use a whip on a slave yourself?" she asked Bathsheba.

149

"I did," Bathsheba admitted, "Once, but not long. It, it was part of my . . . training."

"Training?!" Deb hissed. "Training! That's a dam awful thing to —"

"If I had done back then the way people do now, Deb, I'd have been locked up in a sanitorium for the insane. It . . . wasn't the way of things then. I sorely regret having used that whip now. But if I was back in 1859 again I — but I'm not and I can afford to regret it now."

Mauri and Stan came up the sidewalk then.

"Deb knows," Bathsheba told them. "Zekial told her."

Deb watched for Mauri's and Stan's reaction, which was calm, unperturbed.

"You two believe all this?" Deb asked them, "This — what these two say about comin' from 1859 n' all?"

Stan said yes and Mauri nodded, and Deb backed away from the four of them. "I got to get on home," she said. "I got to think on this." She walked away without saying goodbye, and then turned back. "You all gonna be here tomorrow?" she asked. "None of you plannin' on goin' anywhere else — any time else?"

"We all plan to be here," Mauri answered and Deb left, hunched over and muttering to herself.

"Prentis called this afternoon," Stan told Bathsheba and Zekial on the way to the car. "His dad's much better. He's having a good recovery from the bypass operation."

"Thas good," Zekial said. "Thas real good."

"Yeah. And Prentis says he'll be going back up to the University right after New Year's. One of his roommate's leaving, so you'll be able to stay with him there."

Zekial took a deep breath. "I ain't goin' back down there, Stannie," he said. "I gonna stay up here."

The others made no reply.

"Down there," Zekial continued, "Be harder for me t' think good o' what's comin'. Up hea, I think good o' what's comin' mos' the time. Mos' the time."

"We'll have to talk to my mom about it, Zekial," Stan said.

Zekial nodded. "I think she let me stay with yu, Stannie. But even if she don't, I stayin' up hea somehow. Somehow."

150

The next morning Mauri and Stan stopped Zekial before they entered the mission. Bathsheba and Mrs. Bale had already gone in.

"Zekial," Mauri said, "Stan and I want you to either ignore Bathsheba or be nice to her today."

"That white bish —," Zekial began.

"Just for today. No glaring at her. No muttering. No shoving past her. No hostile announcements. Think you can do it?"

Zekial scowled.

"Listen, Zekial," Stan put in. "Most of the people coming for a meal today have a lot of problems of their own. You'll see them smiling and laughing. But they come because they don't have another place as nice to have a meal on Christmas day.

"Now if you're going to be glaring and muttering at Bathsheba, these people are going to notice it. It'll only confuse them, and it might spoil their enjoyment of this special meal. They're putting aside their troubles today, to come and eat this meal together. And so Mauri and I are asking you to put your troubles aside too, and help make this meal as nice as possible for everybody else."

Zekial had stopped scowling, but he was still frowning. It was as Mauri and Stan had guessed. His disclosures to Deb the day before had made him eager to make his grievances public.

"I try," he finally said. "Jus' for' today, I try. An' only outta r'spec fo' you two and fo' Miz Bale. Not fo' that —"

"We know, we know, Zekial. And thanks," Stan said.

Once inside they were soon put to work and kept very busy. The kitchen hummed with the intense activity. Deb was in there and at close to her maximum clamor, perhaps in part to make up for her lackluster performance the day before.

In the eating rooms the decorations and table arrangements required more effort and concentration than they had for Thanksgiving. A large contingent of Kwanzaa patterns and trimmings were blended in with Christmas decorations and some festive piñatas.

Zekial kept his word to Mauri and Stan. He wasn't nice to Bathsheba, but he did adequately avoid her. Being a new volunteer he was given fairly simple work in the kitchen, and then was asked to help with the setting up in the eating rooms. Deb went out with him and hastily introduced him to Gladys and her husband Mike before returning to the kitchen. He spent much of his time with Gladys and Mike thereafter, moving tables and taping up festoons. Gladys's Georgia voice soothed him wonderfully: her voice, linked to her sweet brown face in the happy bustle of the mission . . . it was like being in the cabins again, in the happier times when they'd gathered over some pilfered sugar and flour and eggs, and laughed about the children's excited hopping and whispering.

How Zekial wished that Mauri could talk like Gladys. How he missed his people in the cabins, the brown women and men who could laugh when they had so little to hope for, when the fear of injustice and separation was always over them. They could be beaten, they could be parted at the whim or mismanagement of their white owners. His mother, his sisters before they — Zekial clouded up suddenly. He had to sit down on one of the folding chairs and cover his eyes with his hands. For him his mother and his sisters were still very much alive in their fears and their sorrows. He missed them terribly. The bustle in the hall went on around him, beyond a quieter space encircling him, and when he was able to bring his head up out of his hands he saw Gladys and Mike, Mauri and Stan standing by him. They were silent. Waiting for him to recover. Waiting for him to join the bustle of the place once more.

He shakily wiped his face off and picked up his roll of tape. Stan slapped him on the back. The preparations went on.

The guests arrived. Zekial helped direct them into seats. He greeted all of his race, trying to say something to put them more at ease. Some of them stared at him as soon as he spoke. Zekial hadn't believed that they would fill up all of the seats in the hall, but they did. More tables and chairs had to be brought in and set up hastily. Zekial stepped back now and then, listening to everyone laughing and joshing each other, and he remembered what Stan had said about all of these people having troubles of their own.

Gladys and Mike saved a seat for him and Deb next to them, and Zekial learned that Mike was Deb's brother and that Gladys was his sister–in–law.

"My sister Deb's a real steady sort," Mike said to Zekial over their meal. "Not at all inclined to hallucinate."

"To . . . what?" asked Zekial.

"To make up things," Gladys put in.

"Yeah," agreed Mike. "That's what I meant. An' she told me and Gladys somethin' last night about you and that Sunrise girl, or whatever her name is."

"S'all be true," Zekial stated.

Gladys tapped Zekial on the shoulder and looked full at him when he turned to her.

"S'all be true," he repeated solemnly.

"Well, I never," Gladys said. "If that don't beat all . . . Mike, you can say I'm crazy, just like you did to Deb, but I . . . I think I believe him too."

Mike didn't say anything. But he put down his knife and fork and wrapped his near arm around Zekial's shoulders. He gave a squeeze and then released Zekial and returned to his meal.

Gladys waited until she saw Bathsheba go back into the kitchen, and got up and followed her, cornering the girl between the stove and trash barrels.

"So your name isn't Sunrise at all," Gladys charged, "and your parents weren't any hip– —"

"You wouldn't have believed me if I'd told you the truth," Bathsheba countered wearily. "But I'm glad you know. What happened to Zekial and his family was . . . was tragic. He deserves all of your sympathy and help, and then some. But I can't go back and change any of it, Gladys. I can only go forward from here."

Gladys shook her head slowly. "How could you?" she asked. "How *could* you —"

"You wouldn't have had much of a choice either, back in 1859. Even in the north, there wasn't much acceptance of the ne– — of the African American."

They talked a little longer, more calmly than Gladys would have thought possible. Then some kitchen workers came in to refill the coffee urns.

Over dessert Gladys hazarded to Zekial, "She say she real sorry, Zekial."

Zekial put down his fork. "I know that," he told Gladys. "Miz Bale already done tol' me that. But it too easy. It all too easy to be sorry *now*. She never sorry back *then*. Never. Now it be too late. Sorry don't mean nothin' now."

153

Gladys nodded and was silent for a while. But before they got up to help clean up, she said quietly. "That's a real big load of hate for you to be carrying around, Zekial. You just be careful now, that it don't carry you down, wear you down. Y'hear?"

Zekial smiled grimly. "I unnerstan'. I be careful," he said, patting her arm. From his history–talking walks with Stan, he knew that the world was finally moving in his direction now. He had only to step into the stream of it and go along with it. Do his part to further it. Enunciating very carefully from memory, he told Gladys, to reassure her, "Let us not seek to satisfy our thirst for freedom by drinking from the cup of bitterness and hatred." But inside himself, he knew that those words from Dr. King's speech had not yet reached his heart.

Part 4 — The seven days of Kwanzaa

Chapter 13

On the day after Christmas the dining room table in the Bale home was set up for celebrating the first day of Kwanzaa.

"Today is the day of unity, of staying together as a people. Umoja!" Stan said as he lit the black candle at the center of the kinara.

Mrs. Bale picked up the kikomba and put it to her lips to sip, but then held the cup out to Zekial.

"You are actually the eldest among us, Zekial," she told him. "You should drink first, and then Bathsheba."

Zekial took the cup and sipped the water. Then he put the cup back onto the mkeka (mat). He would not hand it to Bathsheba.

"It's your turn now, Bathsheba," Mrs. Bale prompted, and Bathsheba took up the cup and sipped from it. She handed it to Mrs. Bale, who sipped and handed the cup to Mauri. From Mauri it went to Stan.

When Stan had placed the cup back on the mkeka, he spoke about what the principle of unity meant to him.

"On the first day of my first Kwanzaa," he said, "I remember looking at my family gathered around the table, and I remember realizing that my father's white face looked . . . out of place. The unity of the first day is supposed to be the unity among African Americans with each other — family unity, community unity . . . it is supposed to mean a united race. It wasn't really intended to express a unity between blacks and whites. So I knew that my father's face didn't belong there, and yet it was there.

"Over the years I grew used to his face at our Kwanzaa table. Unity was a concept, while the color of my father's face was a fact.

"And now my father is no longer here." He paused to regain control of his voice before continuing. "But as I look around the table now, I see another white face. I will never understand how it got here from 1859. But to honor my father, I cannot deny it a place at this table.

"I believe in the unity of the African American people. It was wrong that they were ever enslaved in this country, and it was as terribly wrong that their families were beaten down, divided up and sold. That is what's at the heart of the unity principle for me: we should never forget what happened to our people, and we should unite and be strong together, to honor the memory of those African Americans who were not permitted that basic unity of family and community.

"But for me, unity will always include something more than that. Out of respect for my father, it will always include a white face."

∗   ∗   ∗

The second day of Kwanzaa was a weekday. Mrs. Bale and Stan, Zekial and Bathsheba spent the morning at the New York City Civil Court in Jamaica, Queens.

All of the petitioners' faces that day were brown except Bathsheba's. Most of them were accompanied by several family members or friends, who all stood up in solidarity with the petitioner when he or she was called to the judge's bench.

The courtroom was still full when Zekial's turn came. "Petition of Leroy Smolett," the judge's clerk called out. The Bale's attorney approached the judge's bench, and Stan nudged Zekial. Zekial sprung from his seat and followed the attorney to the bench. Leroy Smolett — that was the name on the birth certificate that Stan had . . . acquired for him.

Bathsheba stood up with Stan and Mrs. Bale when Zekial strode toward the judge, but she sat down again when Zekial turned around at the bench and glared at her.

"What is the name that you have chosen to be known by?" the judge asked Zekial.

"Imani Nia," Zekial answered. "They's Kwanzaa words. Imani mean belief, 'cause I belief in mysef and my people. An' Nia mean . . . it mean I gonna do my bes, so my people an' my friends an' my family, they all be proud o' me."

The judge lingered a little while over Zekial's petition.

"It, well, your new name seems to suit you," she commented.

Zekial made no answer. The judge was white, but Zekial was not afraid. He — Zekial — knew he had the right to be a petitioner in this court.

"Your petition is approved, Mr. Imani Nia," the judge finally said after an awkward pause. Zekial — now Imani — gave the judge a curt, reserved nod before returning to his seat between Mrs. Bale and Stan.

"Sunrise. Sunrise Shansky," the clerk called out, and Bathsheba rose and went before the bench. Behind her Mrs. Bale and Stan again stood up.

"What is the name that you have chosen to known by?" the judge asked.

"Bathsheba Bethay Severly," Bathsheba answered, and the judge regarded her curiously.

"And why, may I ask, have you chosen that name?" she asked.

"They are, um, are names in my family which I, I prefer over the name on my birth documentation," Bathsheba told him.

"The biblical Bathsheba caused a bit of a ruckus in her day, if I remember correctly," the judge commented.

After a moment's pause Bathsheba came back with an oddly impassioned, "She couldn't help who she was. It was, it was the times she lived in. And King Cott — David, I mean King David — she just had to do as he said. She had no choice really."

The judge shook her head, but nonetheless she said, "Your petition is also approved."

That evening Mauri lit the black candle and the red one next to it.

"Today is the day of self–determination," she said. "Kujichagulia. To celebrate the freedom of choice that African Americans now have."

The kikombe was sipped from by everyone as it had been on the day before. Zekial — now Imani — again refused to pass the cup to Bathsheba.

When Stan had placed the cup back on the mkela, Mauri spoke. "I wish that I could have been at the court house with you today, instead of observing an inventory of fish." She wrinkled her nose and smiled wryly before continuing. "By changing their names today, I think that Imani and Bathsheba have both showed what self–determination can mean. Imani picked new names for himself to

157

display his hopes and his determination for the future in a pure and direct way. Bathsheba chose to revert back to her real birth name. When I asked her why she decided to keep it, she told me that she had decided not to run away from who she really is."

* * *

"Ujima!" Mrs. Bale stated as she lit the black candle, the red one lit yesterday and the first green one. "This is the day on which we celebrate how we help each other best by working together."

After the kikombe had been sipped by everyone in turn, Mrs. Bale elaborated on ujima. "To me it means helping each other in the broadest sense," she said. "I myself use this day of Kwanzaa to celebrate a broader charity than that of African Americans helping each other. That was my upbringing, and it is also what I practiced in my years of marriage with my husband."

* * *

Bathsheba lit the previous days' candles plus the next red one.

"This is Ujamaa, the fourth day," Bathsheba said, "to remind African Americans to buy goods from each other."

After the kikombe had been passed around, Bathsheba spoke very briefly. "I think it is good to help others with money when you can, especially for things that they can use to help improve themselves," is all that she said.

* * *

"Nia," Imani said solemnly. "Nia be for day five." He enunciated carefully. He had practiced his speech with Stan, and wanted to sound as much like his hero, Dr. King, as possible. "It means that now we be more free, we all do our best, an' that make my people all the time stronger and better." In his mind Imani saw his house — now almost as large as the Bale's — with its own Kwanzaa celebration. He would have seven children, one for each day of Kwanzaa. He and Mauri would smile at each other over the candles of their kinara. She would have acquired a passable southern inflection in her voice over their years together, and they would both read to all of their children every night. They would live in a friendly, comfortable neighborhood where everyone else was an African American, and he would only buy from African Americans. He would help many African Americans who were less fortunate than

158

himself, with his money and his time, and with his genuine interest and affection. He would live a good life, and always be generous toward his own people.

* * *

All of them except Bathsheba had been invited to celebrate the sixth day of Kwanzaa at Gladys and Mike's house. It had become a big annual party which began at six in the evening, Gladys had explained to Mrs. Bale when she called. Some years it had lasted all night.

"The invitation is really to honor Ze– — I mean Imani," Mrs. Bale told the others. "I've known Deb and Mike's grandmother as an acquaintance for years, but we've never been invited to this before."

"I'll stay home with Bathsheba," she continued.

"I'll stay here by myself," Bathsheba said, "I'll be fine."

But Mrs. Bale shook her head. "I've never liked to be out late on New Year's Eve anyway, Bathsheba," she said. "Too much drinking and partying all round. I prefer to stay home, this year especially."

Mauri didn't say anything, but on the day of the party she deliberately stayed late at the office. It had closed at three p.m., but she and several other auditors stayed on to finish writing up their inventory workpapers.

Mauri called home about five p.m. to tell Stan and Imani to go to the party without her. "I might come later, Stan, but I'll probably just go straight home. I'm just kind of tired."

"Liar," said Stan.

"Yeah," Mauri admitted. There would be drinking at the party, and after a few drinks Imani might get more . . . persistent toward her than he was already. It was best to stay away.

She was filling in her time sheet when Gabriel stopped by her desk. Gabriel was the guy at work that Mauri wasn't quite ready to tell anyone at home about. Mauri sort of liked him, but their conversations had been strictly about business so far. He was about her age, and he had a better sense of humor than most of the accountants she'd met so far. Most recently they'd done the fish inventory together.

"Hey, Mauri, guess what?" Gabriel said as he slid into the chair by her desk. "Taylor wants a recount on the fish job. Right away."

Mauri eyed him carefully.

"You're kidding," she then said calmly, and returned to totaling off her time sheet with an unconcerned air.

"Well, yeah," Gabriel admitted. "But you shoulda seen us last year. Nick did it with me, and he kept getting sick from the, well, the stench of the fish. Turns out he was coming down with something and the smell really got to him. Anyway, Taylor sent me back out on New Year's Eve last year with a senior named Barbara to recheck the whole thing."

"Wow. The whole thing?"

"Yeah. Taylor kept saying that he didn't mind fishy workpapers, but barfy workpapers just hit too close to home."

"Oh, God, what a comic."

"Yeah, he manages to crack a joke every other year or so."

"So how long did it take to recheck the inventory?"

"Not nearly as long as I'd expected. Barbara had a date and the warehouse men were pretty eager to start their New Year's celebrations too. She started barking at them the moment we got there, and they scurried around like crazy to keep up with her. Then she got furious near the end because she realized that she stunk of fish — you know how it gets in your hair and everything?"

"Oh, yeah," Mauri drawled.

"Yeah, and so she started swearin' and — because she was going to have to go home and scrub and change instead of going straight from the job to meet her boyfriend like she'd planned."

"And she didn't get in trouble for swearing at the client's employees?"

"In trouble?! Hell — heck, no, Mauri. Those guys loved it. I think she may have even taught them a few, er, combinations that they hadn't thought of before."

Mauri and Gabriel laughed companionably.

"You never met Barbara," Gabriel continued. "See, she works for that client now, down in the Baltimore office."

"Oh?"

"Yeah. Turns out that one of the guys that she was bossing around and cussing out had come up from the Baltimore office to keep an eye on things. When we got there I just introduced her to the foreman and she went right to, ah, work. We thought that the

160

Baltimore guy was just another worker — he looked like 'em, talked like 'em . . . hey, would you like to go out to dinner with me?"

"Now?! Tonight?!"

"Well, sure."

They went to a small restaurant near the office. They enjoyed themselves, talking comfortably about many things. Mauri hadn't intended to tell Gabriel about Bathsheba and Imani, but over coffee at the end of the meal she changed her mind.

Gabriel was incredulous, of course. But he did not out and out disbelieve it, after sizing up how Mauri described everything, and her willingness to let him meet them and decide what he thought of them for himself.

"So this guy Imani," Gabriel asked her soon after she finished telling him, "he really likes you a lot?"

Mauri answered carefully. "He's bound to change his mind about me. It may have already begun to happen. I just don't want to let him down in, in the meantime. He's kind of a powerful dreamer —"

"I'll say!"

"Yeah, and he needs his dreams a lot, just to get by right now."

* * *

When the phone rang at the Bale residence about eight p.m. Bathsheba answered it.

"Is this Bathsheba Bethay Severly?" a male voice asked.

Bathsheba recognized the voice. "Speaking," she said. "Why have you called me, Officer Welson?"

"I'm not calling as an officer of the law," was the response. "I'm calling as a . . . as an acquaintance."

"Does that mean that I'm not likely to be arrested by you any time soon?" Bathsheba asked.

They talked for half an hour. After Bathsheba hung up she found Mrs. Bale in the living room and told her about the call.

"He said he'll be starting law school in the Fall," Bathsheba finished up. "And that he hopes we can keep up an, an acquaintance of, of some, of some sort."

"Well," said Mrs. Bale over her knitting, "that sounds like a . . . start."

Bathsheba nodded and leaned back into the couch and closed her eyes.

"How's the studying coming?" Mrs. Bale asked.

"I'm all done in for tonight," Bathsheba replied yawning. "I always do better early in the morning, anyway."

"Your exam date's coming up pretty fast. And Stan hasn't been able to help you as much as he originally intended."

"Oh, he's still helped me a great deal. So have you and Mauri. And I'm doing okay on the self–testing so far. I think I'll make it."

Mrs. Bale nodded.

"I wonder how Stan and Imani are doing at that party," Bathsheba mused.

* * *

When Stan and Imani arrived at the party at about seven o'clock, it was already in full swing. Talking, laughing people of all ages were everywhere, and lively drum–driven music boomed from an awesome sound system.

"This is Nancy, my baby sister," Gladys told Stan and Imani over the music, soon after they arrived. "She and my mom are up from Savannah for the rest of the week."

Nancy was a college junior. "Gladys told me and mom about you, Imani," she said shyly.

"An' does yu belief her?" Imani asked. He was nervous with so many people around, and he unconsciously reverted to his older way of talking.

"I didn't at first, but by now I almost do. Mainly because Gladys and Deb are so straight — they just couldn't have made something like you up. So, would you mind telling me about some of it, about what it was like to have been a slave?"

Imani easily sensed that there was still a considerable amount of disbelief in the girl. That was perfectly natural, he knew. He wouldn't have believed it either, if it hadn't happened to him.

He would have preferred to be a 1990s party goer for a while, and to just absorb what was going on around him and enjoy himself. Maybe get a little lightheaded on some wine or some whiskey. But the girl had asked him about his history, and he took her request very

162

seriously. She was also pleasant to be with. Her voice was pretty, her face was comely and her eyes were beautiful.

"I do my bes'," he told her, and the three of them — Imani, Stan and Nancy — sat down at the far end of the dining room, where the music was not quite as loud.

Imani spoke with Nancy for a very long time, answering her questions, and telling her things that he thought she should know. Stan left once or twice and brought back some fresh sodas, and once some wine for the three of them. Imani was working hard trying to explain his experiences, and the girl was very interested. Stan helped, often suggesting a word or phrase that Imani seemed to be searching for.

Imani was so intent on making slavery real for Nancy that he did not really notice how the boisterous party had gradually quieted. He did not notice when the music was turned down and then off. He thought maybe he'd been talking way too long and that the party had somehow ended without him realizing it. It was completely silent behind him. Nancy in front of him had tears on her face and Stan's head was bowed with emotion. Imani decided that he would check about what happened to the party as soon as he finished what he was saying.

"An' dat de las' time I see Jacob alive."

Imani turned around then, and saw with a jolt of surprise that the room was full of silent people, all looking straight at him. For a few moments he thought that they were the ghosts of his ancestors, standing motionless in their African–patterned garb. They looked so sad, and some of them had tears like Nancy. "Don't be so sad!" he wanted to tell them, but he was afraid to break the immense silence. He sat rigid and small before them, breathing unevenly.

Then a stocky man stepped from the crowd and seized Imani's hands. "That was . . . the most profound oration on . . . on slavery that I, I have ever . . ." The man could not finish. He sobbed over Imani's hands.

Gladys and Mike stepped from the crowd and began to comfort the man. "Gladys!" the man sobbed when he could speak again, "Mike! That was just . . . outstanding! So real. So moving. Where on earth did you find such an accomplished actor? And such material? I will never, ever forget it for as long as I live."

A woman in the crowd then spoke up. "Marvin speaks for all of us," she said shakily. The crowd then burst into a roaring murmur, sprung from the spell of Imani's heartfelt words. A number of people surged toward Imani to talk to him, but all he wanted to do was to hide from them. It was too much for him. He was suddenly drained, exhausted. He was confused, muddled. Nancy noticed and whispered to Stan, and together she and Stan slipped Imani outside to the patio. There Imani began to relax, and his mind gradually cleared. He knew that he had done something important, and had done it well. He only wished that Mauri had come and that she could hear what everyone was saying about him.

Gladys and Mike found them a short while later. "You must be getting a bit cold out here by now," Gladys said. "Come on in now for the lighting of the kinara. Zek— — ah, Imani, we'd be honored if you would light our kinara for us this evening."

Imani demurred, but Stan and Nancy encouraged him. "Just be yourself," Nancy urged him softly, and Imani found himself lighting the beautifully carved kinara with her nearby, smiling at him, before he fully realized what he was doing.

"Today we celebrate Kuumba," Imani said quietly, shy in front of all the people. "We take whut we haf, an' we clever with it as we can be. Better times for' all o' our people that way."

While the kikombe cups were being passed around the drummers arrived. Gladys rushed to the door to meet them.

"Law I thought you all weren't ever gonna get here!" everyone could hear her saying. "But you're just in time. Start up just as soon as you can. Everybody's *ready*."

Everybody *was* ready. From the first drum beats their bodies were bobbing, swaying, willing and eager for the dancing. It had been a great party, and then what they had heard from Imani had deeply moved them. Now came the time to express their feelings of happiness and awe. They were ready to honor and celebrate their heritage and themselves in their dance.

Each dancer's enthusiasm fed an odd frenzy. It was exuberant and wild. The drummers noticed this right away and exchanged glances. They smiled thinly among themselves, very smug. 'So these people want to dance?' they telegraphed to each other in their glances

164

and in their initial drumbeats. 'Alright. Let's stretch 'em.' They intensified their beat and drove it on.

The dancers did not disappoint them. They responded readily, joyously. The drums and the spirits of the dancers joined together on this night, in this memorable celebration.

Stan and Nancy were new to this kind of dancing, but some of it was vaguely familiar to Imani. The three of them just bobbed at first. Gradually they tried out some of the steps that they saw the others doing, and soon they were dancing competently, if simply.

Now and then Imani took a break from dancing, with either Stan or Nancy. He had imbibed some liquor and was feeling wonderful. How different all of this was from the Christmas week dancing that he'd done as a slave. Then he'd danced with a hollow feeling, seizing the small respite from the whites' demands, knowing that the interlude would soon be over, knowing that they really had nothing to celebrate at all.

And now here he was dancing with real hope, with real pleasure. An amazingly free man, among people that liked him, even admired him. He knew that he had never been as happy as this in his entire life.

And yet tears would fall from his eyes, sometimes, while he danced. Right after New Years the master always sold off some of the slaves. Only last New Year's Day his youngest sister had been sold to a dealer heading west to Mississippi. His poor little sister, who had only been ten. Dancing and laughing with him during the week after Christmas. Surely she would not be sold, they had thought. She was so useful to Takita in the kitchen, and she always did more than her portion in the fields.

But then she was gone, prodded irretrievably down the road behind the slave trader's wagon, wailing and shrieking that New Year's Day. Mother had fallen into the dirt and just cried and cried. She cried for days and days, and aged considerably after that. Her baby, her youngest, torn from her like all of the others except Zekial. Her heart broken again and yet again.

The dancing at Gladys's and Mike's house went on late into the night, and well into the early hours of the next morning. The drummers, having accepted the challenge of these unusually passionate and exuberant dancers, played in shifts to keep the drumming well–nigh continuous.

Imani didn't remember exactly when he fell asleep. He had been determined to keep up with the dancing, but was having to take more and more breaks from it. He had sat down on one end of a long deep sofa and Nancy had sat down very close beside him. They were sipping their sodas in a tired, peaceful silence, watching the crowd of dancers. The crowd was thinning somewhat, but there were still a lot of dancers going at it strong. Most of the children were no longer dancing — many of them were sprawled on the furniture or along the walls, asleep or drowsing or talking idly.

The patterns on the clothes of the dancers began to bob and swirl before Imani's eyes, oddly disembodied from the dancing bodies. The beat of the drums drove deep into his brain.

Then he saw his youngest sister dancing in the crowd, almost naked in her dull thin shift, but flopping and whirling happily, carefree. She didn't know yet, Imani realized. She thought she'd be kept on, that she was safe from the soul drivers for sure.

Then Imani saw Mauri standing among the dancing people, standing stock still the way she'd been when he'd first met her — just before he'd bumped into her and knocked her down into the red Georgia mud, with Bathsheba's harangue driving him on, driving him out of his muzzy dream and into her. How stiff Mauri looked, just standing there among the supple dancing bodies.

He remembered the dream that Bathsheba had startled him out of when she found him dozing in the woodshed, and he remembered the promise that Bette had made to him. For hiding her from the pater rollers, at no small risk to himself, she had arranged her magic so that the next time he dreamed sweetly he would get what he dreamed of.

"Dream yu somethin' good t' eat, Zekial. Or dream yu a purty womun yu be wantin'," she whispered to him, with an ugly cackle. "Dream yu shoes an' a fine jackit. Yu git it," she'd promised him. "Yu git it."

"Whut 'bout ma freedom?" Zekial had asked her, but she'd laughed at him about that.

"Whoa! Ha!" she'd cackled, almost falling into him in her mirth. "I ain't got dat much conjurin', Zekial! I sho ain't got dat much ! Yu tink I be hea mysef on dis hea place, if'n I did? Ha!"

But Zekial had wanted to dream of freedom anyway, of escape, and of an end to the white man's rule.

Now as Imani, a free man in Gladys's and Mike's living room he slept deeply, and he did not wake up until the air freshened markedly. It must be morning, he thought groggily. It always smells like this around about dawn on a cold winter morn.

He dragged his eyes open and blinked. He was not in anybody's living room any more. He was prone on a bed of brown pine needles in the small tent–like area under a pine tree's lowest branches. The branches were just above his head, and they bent down to the ground at the tree's perimeter. He hadn't slept under a tree like this since he was a small child.

Nancy was curled up in front of him and Stan was at his back. He slid out from between them carefully, so as not to wake them, but they were already stirring anyway. He crawled out between two of the low branches of their pine bower, his head pounding remarkably. He dared not stand up yet, lest his head split wide open.

The world out from under the pine tree was a totally green world, except for an amazingly blue sky overhead. Pine trees stretched in even rows for as far as he could see. The world was hushed: there was no sound at all except a bare whisper of pine needles in a very light breeze. No birds, Imani thought worriedly. And no little critters scurrying across the ground and through the trees.

Cold pressed against his face and hands, and entered his knees through the cloth of his jeans. The air was fresh and startlingly pure.

Stan nudged himself out from under the tree on one side of Imani, and Nancy ventured out on his other side. Like him, they were not prepared to lift their heads above their crawling positions yet.

"Zek– — I mean Imani," Stan said woozily, "what is this? Where are we?"

"I don' know, Stannie," Imani whispered back. Their voices sounded very strange to him in the utter stillness of the place. "I don' know," he repeated. "All I knows is that I wuz havin' a dream —"

"A dream?!" Stan asked quickly — too quickly, and gasped and rubbed the back of his head. Imani winced in sympathy for him.

"A . . . dream," Stan repeated more carefully. Then with a look of surprise and alarm, "A dream! Ohmygod . . . Imani! What have you done? Where have you taken us?"

"Stannie!" Imani replied worriedly. "I don' . . . I jus' don' know!"

The three of them gradually helped each other into walking upright, offering each other an arm to lean on, or a shoulder or leg to brace against for balance at the critical times. Imani was glad he hadn't drunk more than he did, else he was sure his head would have simply rolled off into the sparse grass. It didn't, though. It stayed on his shoulders, though just barely, and it pained him very much indeed.

By the time he was thinking these thoughts they were wandering slowly among the precise rows of pine trees.

Nancy shuddered. "I don't believe I like this place very much," she said. "It's real pretty and all, and so quiet and green. But it reminds me of . . . of a cemetery somehow. These trees are spaced too even, I think. Way too even."

"It's the sky that's bothering me," Stan said. "It just doesn't look real to me."

The three of them then gazed at the sky. "It looks sort of . . . tinted." Nancy said at last, squinting.

"Yes," agreed Stan, "like it's —"

"Whut dat?" Imani said suddenly, and the others froze and listened with him.

A soft whirring sound came to them, as if from very far away. They turned toward the sound and gradually it got more distinct, though it was still very low pitched and quiet. Then they could see something coming toward them from far off, between two long rows of trees. It came slowly, and eventually resolved itself into a someone in a spacesuit, riding on something that looked like the basket of a shopping cart. The vehicle skimmed the ground without wheels or rails.

The rider in the spacesuit was a man, a large brown–skinned man. They all sensed right away that he was friendly. All of his movements were calm, carefully nonthreatening. He got out of his

. . . cart, and handed each of them a small thin plastic square, about the size of a CD case.

The stranger held a similar square, and he pressed some touch pads on it. Tiny lights flashed and raced in unison across the surfaces of all four squares. Then he gestured at them to speak to him.

"Ah, hey dere," Imani volunteered.

"Um, we're peaceful," Stan said.

"Dat's so," Imani put in. "We frens."

"Who are you?" asked Nancy wonderingly. "What is this place?"

The man smiled kindly at them and pressed the touch pads of his square some more. Corresponding lights on their squares blipped and raced. Then the man spoke. His words were unintelligible to them, but as he spoke a voice came from each of their squares in a bizarre computer chorus, and they could understand what the crisp voices were saying.

"Do you have names?" the voices in the squares asked them in unison. "If you do, what are they?"

They each spoke their names to the man in turn.

"I couldn't find some of Imani's language in the lingual archives," the voices continued as the man spoke to them, somewhat apologetically, "so I've programmed our translators for the closest amalgam of Nancy's and Stan's dialects. Is this understandable by all three of you?"

They nodded.

"Good," the voices continued when the man spoke again. "Then we can communicate. Entry sensors picked you up when you arrived, and I came as soon as I could get into my autoimmune suit." The man turned to Nancy. "You asked who I was and where you were. I am Hua, and you are inside the Dome of the Memorial Forest for the Great Eradication."

"Ah, excuse me," Stan said, eyeing the man's vehicle and the thin plastic squares in their hands, "but what year is this, please?"

"You speak in terms of years," the chorus of accentless computer voices responded. "That is a rather archaic unit of measure. But let me see if I can . . ." Hua pressed his touch pads and lights raced across his square.

"You're — you're reading those light flashes," Stan said, stunned by the idea.

169

Hua smiled and nodded amiably. "Of course."

'Damn,' thought Imani. 'Another language I'll have to learn!' He felt that he was having enough trouble already with English. 'Damn.'

"In terms of years," the voices then informed them, "it is now the year 2120."

Imani, Nancy and Stan stared stupidly at Hua. Then, "I was afraid it would be something like this," Stan muttered softly.

"Oh, you should have nothing to fear," the voices told them as Hua spoke his unintelligible words to them. "The Great Eradication is long over. Our victory was complete. Peace and prosperity will be ours for many . . . well, let's just say for many, many years to come."

"An' whut," Imani asked, "whut wuz dis hea Great Rad'cation?" Hua frowned slightly at his translator. "Pardon me, Imani," the voices said, "But your language is . . . you want to know what the Great Eradication was, perhaps?" Hua guessed, and Imani nodded.

"It was a complex event," the voices spoke, "with a complex build up. But in very basic terms, it was caused by a cadre of neo—racist white guerilla warriors. Under —"

"Wait now, su," said Imani. "What's a neo —"

"That would be white bigots, Imani," Stan put in.

Hua continued when Imani nodded. "Under the leadership of a madman, this group terrorized nonwhites — African Americans, Hispanics, Native Americans, Asians. They were extremely vicious and . . . quite effective — far out of proportion to their small numbers.

"Efforts to stamp them out were never entirely successful, and then . . . let's see, that would have been the year . . . 2105. In 2105 their terrorism began to get some broader based support. Other whites began to join them in greater numbers. There was some very clever manipulation going on, and the more neutral whites began to feel threatened by what appeared to be backlash hostilities by nonwhites. More and more of them began to side with the guerillas and, ultimately, the decision to eradicate was made."

"The decision to . . ." Stan asked faintly. "Ah, what exactly was erad—, eradicated?"

"It is not a question of what," the voices in the squares replied softly as Hua spoke, "but of who."

"Who, then?" Stan asked.

170

"All of the whites," the voices said.

"Some of it was unfortunate," they continued. "There were quite a number of whites who had been working and fighting with us, against the neo–racist scourge. But they had to be eradicated along with the others of their race. And we lost many of mixed racial ancestry too — all of those with a relatively high proportion of whiteness in them. That part of the eradication was particularly tragic."

"But how was an, an entire race eradicated?" Stan asked. He was swaying oddly, Imani noticed. Imani grabbed his arm to steady him.

"Targeted negative gene dispersals, essentially," the voices replied.

Stan lurched forward blindly, despite Imani's hold on his arm.

"I feel . . . odd," he said weakly. His translator square slipped from his fingers and fell to the ground, and he dropped heavily to his knees.

"Stannie!" Imani cried out, going down with him and holding him by his shoulders. "Stannie!"

"What's happening?!" Nancy wailed shakily. "What's happening to Stan?"

"He's a mixed race then, isn't he?" the voices asked as Hua spoke. "I had noticed a few characteristics — but I'd rather hoped that he wouldn't succumb to the — unfortunately there's still a significant amount of the dispersal agent in the air.

"I'm sorry for you, Nancy and Imani," the voices continued as Hua spoke and looked on sadly, "since you obviously care for your friend. But do not worry about his comfort. His end will be swift and humane. He is probably already —"

"No! Stannie!" Imani screamed. "Stannie, don' die!"

"Imani," Nancy said coolly, "Imani, wake up."

"But Nancy, Stannie — Stannie is —"

"Wake up Imani," Nancy repeated calmly. "You've been having a real bad dream, honey."

"Du– dream?" Imani asked woozily. He was totally confused, but struggling now for coherence, to comprehend what reality was, and what it wasn't.

171

"Yeah, you been dreamin'. So wake on up now." Imani felt Nancy's hand on his arm. "But whatever you do," she continued, "don't get up too fast, y'hear?"

"Uhhhh . . . 'kay," Imani said, awake enough now to be extra careful about how he moved his head. "But where Stannie? Is he okay? Is he okay? He ain't dead?"

"He's curled up right over there on the floor, beside that armchair. And he ain't dead," Nancy replied sympathetically.

Imani risked opening his eyes. He was still in Gladys's and Mike's living room, one of a number of horizontally inclined, groggy males. Gladys was in the doorway, hands on her hips. A little stern but not angry.

Nancy grinned at Imani. "I've got to go now," she told him. "Gladys hauled me outta here when the dancing stopped, and she only let me back in 'cause you were yellin' in your sleep and we got, well, we got a little concerned about you."

"There's a help–yourself breakfast in the kitchen when you all is ready," Gladys announced before she and Nancy left the room.

Chapter 14

Stan and Imani arrived home around noon and got cleaned up and changed. Soon afterward everyone in the household got into the car for the drive to the woods.

Every year on New Year's Day the Bale family had visited Mangaru, a small nature preserve in Westchester county, to celebrate the seventh day of Kwanzaa in the woods. Rain, snow and tv football games had never deterred them, even in the days before VCR time shifting entered their home.

This year Imani and Bathsheba accompanied Mrs. Bale, Mauri and Stan. And they also stopped by Gladys and Mike's house to pick up Nancy, whom Stan and Imani had invited that morning.

Imani was unusually quiet in the car and during the walk through the woods to the waterfall. He was thinking a lot about the dream he had had — about 2120 when there were no more whites in the world. The air was cool and crisp in the woods, like in his dream, but the trees here were very pleasantly irregular and haphazardly placed. He rejoiced in that, and in the erratic crackling of withered leaves under his warm sturdy boots.

In his mind his children were with him and they ran laughing through these leaves, their jackets bright splashes of color against the winter brown hillside that they were scrambling up. Then in another moment he was imagining their grandchildren — his great grandchildren — running down the silent aisles of gnarled old pine trees in the Memorial Forest under the Dome, their musical voices the only sounds for miles and miles. But for that to happen, they could have no white blood in them . . .

His thoughts shifted fluidly back to the images of his children running through these woods. He knew that he would select those bright–colored jackets for them with the same meticulous care that he used for selecting his own beloved attire. His wife Mauri — or was that really Mauri who was running back and forth among the children? Her face was turned away from him and her profile wasn't quite what he had thought it would be. And somehow the laugh was not quite her laugh . . .

All of the laughter in his mind — his, his children's, his wife's — was in the leaves scattered by the wind and by his boots. Perhaps that accounted for some of the distortion of Mauri's laugh, he thought. Perhaps . . .

Mrs. Bale stopped at a fork in the rough upward path and said to the others, "Not much farther." For the benefit of Imani, Bathsheba and Nancy, she continued. "This all used to be part of an abandoned quarry. It was heavily eroded and used as a local dump. Then it was bought by a retired couple who spent years and all of their spare money, to turn it into a nature preserve."

They ate sandwiches by the small waterfall at the end of the high path, and then they set up their Kwanzaa table on a flat rock that was close by. Nancy lit all seven of the candles in order.

"Today is the last day of Kwanzaa," she said softly. "The day of Imani, of faith. Today we celebrate our belief in ourselves. Today we hold our heads up especially high, because we know that we are worthy of everyone's respect.

Imani picked up the kikombe and sipped from it. He held it in his hands, staring down into it. Then he thrust it abruptly at Bathsheba and turned away with furious tears falling from his eyes. The water in the cup sloshed violently over Bathsheba's fingers, and Bathsheba almost dropped the cup in her surprise. But it was done. He had done what the spirit of Kwanzaa asked of him. His belief in himself and in his people had just become strong enough. But only just.

Bathsheba sipped from the cup shakily and passed it on. When everyone had sipped and the cup had been placed back on the mkela, Nancy spoke of what Imani meant to her. Then the group fell silent, and watched the candles burn brighter and brighter in the rapidly dimming light.

"I'd like to tell you all 'bout the dream I had this mornin'," Imani said to the others, staring at the candles' flames. And while the candles burned down, one by one into darkness, he related it.

"Well," said Mrs. Bale quietly into the darkness when he had finished. "I'm glad that was only a dream, Imani."

174

"Yeah," Imani replied. "some o' it anyway. I wouldn't ever want to lose ol' Stannie."

"Thanks, man" Stan said, and he slapped Imani affectionately on the back.

They turned on their flashlights and made their way back down the trail. Mrs. Bale was happy for the young people. Imani in particular seemed to be making remarkable strides. But she was also sad. This was her first Kwanzaa and New Year's without her husband, and she missed him keenly. Mauri and Bathsheba stayed close to her. Between them they had been drawing her out whenever she became too quiet and withdrawn. Mauri was also delicately keeping herself clear of Imani, to give Nancy a clear field for his affection. Now she concentrated on playing her flashlight ahead for her mother's steps, and wondered a little about what Gabriel might be doing just then.

Bathsheba had always felt more secure with Mrs. Bale than with anyone else she had met since she left 1859. It was such a very strange — and sometimes hostile — world to her, even though she had choices now which she could never have dreamed of before. And on top of the rest of the strangeness — what she thought of now as the ordinary strangeness — she also had to quell the sometimes intense waves of attraction that she felt toward Stan. Stan had given her no encouragement. He had clearly signaled to her that any affection she had for him would not be reciprocated. That had helped. But it was Stan's mother who provided the strength for bearing with the hopeless longing. Mrs. Bale had been a true friend to her, and Bathsheba returned that friendship with her own love and solicitude.

Stan, Nancy and Imani kept with each other on the path down the hill. They felt all the closer, for having been together in Imani's affecting dream. They sailed down through the fragile leaves in the darkness, moving almost by feel. They felt nearly invincible, like carefree children. They plied their flashlight beams across each other's jackets and jeans. But there were undertones, invisible tendrils fluttering between them, dragging across a sleeve, tickling the neck or cheek hairs in a richly exciting way. Imani and Stan were fully conscious of how attractive Nancy was, and of how . . . much more alluring she became as she slipped past the weak rods of their torch

175

beams. And Nancy laughed musically, beguilingly to them both in the darkness beyond them. Somewhere in this was the unadulterated joy of their youth, and the three of them well knew it. Risks as well, of course. But they would reach for the joy. They would have it. The future was theirs. They would seize it and would take as much of it with them as was possible, into a golden old age.

www.ingramcontent.com/pod-product-compliance
Lightning Source LLC
Chambersburg PA
CBHW032011170626
46807CB00006B/2754